# TESSILI
## REVENGE

# BOOKS BY ROBIN STEPHEN

**Chronicles of the Tessilari**
*Tessili Academy*
*Tessili Rogue*
*Tessili Revenge*

**Annals of the Brinlocks**
*Brinlin Isle*
*Brinlin Forest*
*Brinlin Cove*

# Tessili Revenge

*Chronicles of the Tessilari: Book III*

Robin Stephen

BROWN WING
PRESS

This is a work of fiction. All characters, events, and organization
portrayed in this novel are either product's of the author's imagination
or are used fictitiously.

TESSILI REVENGE

Copyright © 2015 by Brown Wing Press

robinstephen.com

ISBN 978-0-9844912-7-8 (ebook)
ISBN 978-0-692-51999-8 (print)

Cover design by Robin Deutschendorf
Maps by Robin Deutschendorf

Brown Wing Press
Iowa City, IA
brownwingpress.com

First Brown Wing Press Edition

*for my sister, the very first to love my tall tales*

ELYS YINS

NELYNA
(FOG ISLES)

CARREG DINAS
GOL LEDRITH
LAN DINAS

TWO TRIALS

SERPEN

SHI

N

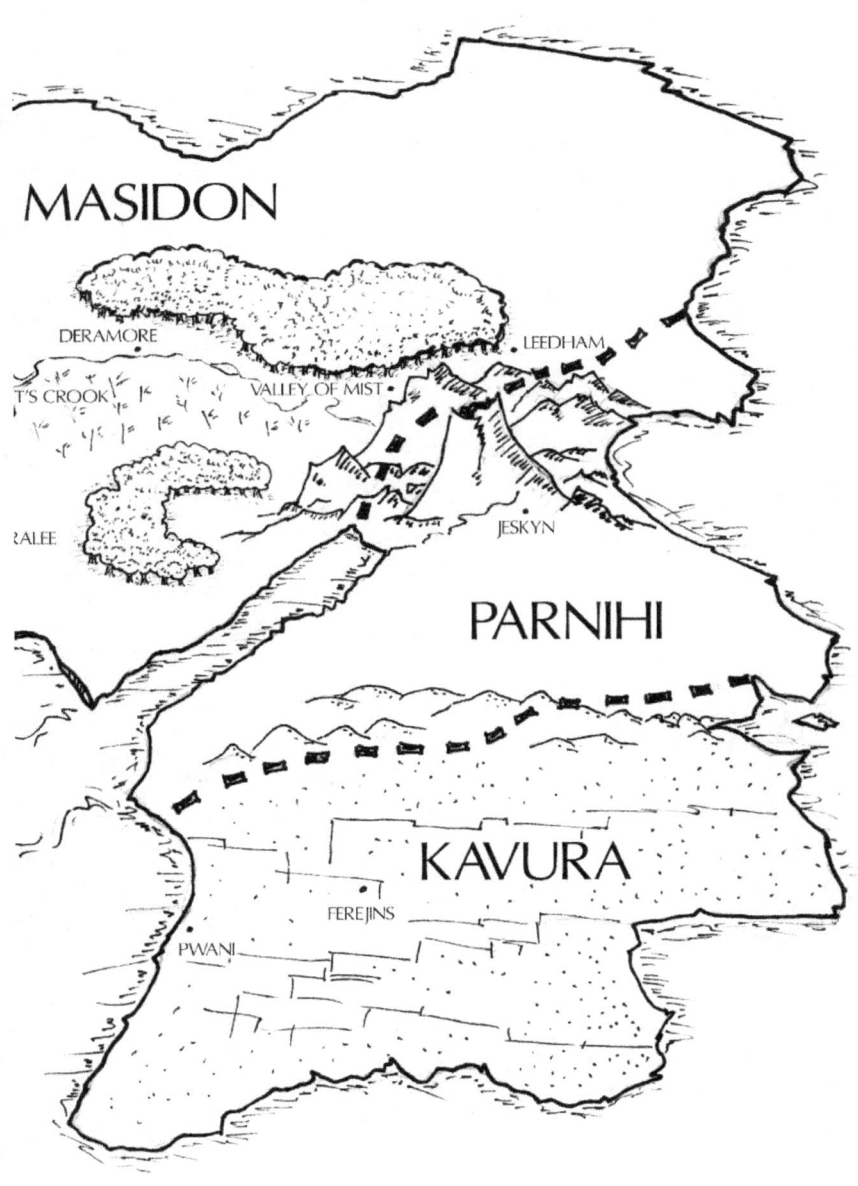

BYDAIRA

MASIDON

DERAMORE

T'S CROOK

VALLEY OF MIST

LEEDHAM

RALEE

JESKYN

PARNIHI

KAVURA

FEREJINS

PWANI

# CHAPTER 1

First Mage Otha sat in her private greenhouse, chair oriented so the unbroken sunlight poured through the windows onto her face. The day was young. Though the dry wind carried a sharp edge as it blew down from the frosted peaks, here among the brillbane the air was warm.

Still, Otha had a woolen blanket spread across her lap. It seemed she was never quite warm anymore. She supposed such were the consequences of living for over 400 years.

There was a rustling near the entryway, and a murmur of voices. First Mage Otha suppressed a sigh. She had agreed, again, to meet with High Mage Agina, even though they both knew their conversation would doubtless play out in a manner no different from all the times before.

Otha composed herself. She sat a little straighter in her chair, trying to draw optimism and strength from the gentle warmth of the sunbeam. Grip, sensing her anxiety, fluttered over from his favorite brillbane perch to settle on his preferred spot on the back of her right hand. He glanced up, his black eyes shrewd and a little worried.

The tessila's scales were still as brilliant a purple as ever, but he, too, was showing signs of age. Several scales along his brow ridge had shed out only to grow in flat black instead of incandescent purple. These days, Grip never ventured far from Otha's side. Being apart made both of them anxious.

More murmuring drifted in from the hall. Willis appeared, looking flustered as usual. "High Mage Agina will see you now, if you're ready, my lady."

Otha waved a thin hand and the young man withdrew. Otha closed her eyes. Grip settled down, shifting his stiff joints so his soft belly was snugged up against her worn skin.

There was the tap of shoes and the rustle of fabric as Agina entered and settled into the chair opposite Otha. For a moment, Otha considered keeping her eyes closed – letting them think she'd drifted off to sleep. They all thought her half senile anyway. She wasn't, of course. She just found it increasingly difficult to care about the mundane conflicts they so often brought to her to resolve.

But she knew why Agina had come today. She also knew the other woman wouldn't leave until they'd spoken. With tired reluctance, she opened her eyes.

The High Mage sat upright and rigid in her chair. Her tessila, Fara, sat on her knee, wings tucked back and chin held aloft. They'd both always been a bit proud.

"Hello, Agina." Although Otha's skin was thin and her eyes watery, her voice was still strong. She was glad of that. It wouldn't do for the First Mage to speak in wavering tones.

Agina didn't waste time with pleasantries. She rarely did. "We have authorized a party to leave the valley. They will collect intelligence regarding the current state of affairs at Tessili Academy, and infiltrate the court. We need to know more about public sentiment in the current culture to make informed decisions."

Otha said nothing. Grip settled a little lower on her hand, growing drowsy. Otha could remember a time he'd have bristled just at having another tessila in his territory. She supposed age had mellowed them both.

There was a long silence. Outside, a breeze was blowing the tops of the pine trees, making them wave and bend in fitful bobs. In the greenhouse, all was still.

Agina shifted, and continued. "It's our hope there might be less fear in the populace now. So much time has passed, after all."

Beyond the pine trees, the mountains reared. From her vantage, Otha could only see their snow-blanketed shoulders. The peaks, she knew, reached high into the bright sky – jagged tops raking at the heavens. At their base hung the mists, thick and heavy. Otha could feel the trickle of thought and energy that spell took from her. She'd been helping to hold the mists in place since the day they'd been summoned.

She understood the hope that drove the younger people to search for a way out. She couldn't deny the Tessilari were slowly dying in this place. When they'd settled here, everyone had feared the population would outgrow this valley. Now, houses stood abandoned at the ends of streets. In the 384 years since the remnants of the Tessilari had found refuge in this place, the tessili they'd brought with them had thrived briefly, then begun to fail. And so the Tessilari failed as well.

Otha understood the hope, yes, but she didn't share it. She closed her eyes again, feeling the vast loneliness that came with an unusually long life. She was the only living Tessilari who remembered – who had seen the people of Masidon go mad. She'd seen the men and women who'd fought beside her in the long, brutal War of the Diods turn the weapons the Tessilari had created for use against a common enemy back on those who'd made them. So much of her long life had faded in her mind—the faces of her loved ones, the tenor of her own mother's voice—but she remembered those terrible days when man had fought man, brother had betrayed brother, and, at last, the Tessilari had fled.

So she understood High Mage Agina's reasons for pushing. She even sympathized. But she couldn't agree with the decision. She met the younger woman's sharp gaze. It was the curse of the old, to know so much and be so little regarded. Oh, they pretended to respect her. But they no longer heeded what she said.

First Mage Otha did the only thing she could do. She repeated what she'd been saying for centuries. She spoke with the conviction only one granted the sight could claim when speaking about the future. "Our moment will come," she said. "If we wait."

High Mage Agina's lips compressed in an expression of frustration. She didn't understand. She didn't truly believe in the sight, just as a man without hearing cannot believe in music. First Mage Otha was the last of the Tessilari who possessed this particular gift. There was no one left who understood her.

Agina let out a slow breath, and stood. She was disappointed. Well, so was Otha. The First Mage responded with only the barest of nods as the younger woman took her leave and walked out of the room.

Otha settled back onto her cushions. She closed her eyes. She wasn't trying to *see*, but she did anyway. A face rose up behind her eyes. It was a face as familiar as even her own, so often she'd seen it. And it was not a nice face.

Eyes closed, sun warm on her skin, Otha *saw* what she'd seen so many times in her 403 years of life. She saw the man, face twisted into a scowl, walking with a pronounced limp, leading the thin, grubby child on a leash towards ….

She could never see what. She could never see why. She could never see when.

Such were the limitations of the sight. She only knew this man, whoever he was, would deliver their moment. If only the Tessilari would wait.

◈

Jey swung her staff at Treyam's head, keeping her balance distributed between her two feet. As she expected, Treyam stepped back. In the moment of his movement, she ducked, let go of one end of the staff, and sent a ferocious swipe towards his knees. Just for practice, she knit a quick active force spell and dropped it onto the staff. She felt the velocity of her swing increase.

The staff, carved all over in a filigree of ancient runes, hummed with magic. It was an ancient weapon, beautifully crafted. The stone it had been made from somehow altered to be hard as iron, light as bamboo, and very receptive to magic. She'd discovered how to make it burn in her hands, how to back it up with deadly force, and how to call it to her from as far away as she could get. The staff was the sort of thing Jey had hoped to find in the Valley of Mist when she'd first arrived.

Unfortunately, it was not hers. The staff belonged to Treyam. There were only six such weapons in the valley. Treyam had inherited his from his father, who had been given it by his father before him. It was a treasured and revered artifact of a time when the Tessilari had been a different sort of people.

Jey had no hope of getting one of her own. The art of making such things was lost.

The staff, fortunately, was also enchanted so it could not harm one of its own blood. Still, Jey had not learned to trust the thing entirely. Even while her heart beat a little faster and her blood pounded in her veins, adrenaline singing in her system as she imagined the blow that swing would have delivered had it been leveled against a true opponent, she pulled the staff at the last moment and only tapped lightly on Treyam's knees.

The young man collapsed into the grass anyway, laughing in mock defeat. Jey straightened, setting the end of the staff on the ground. For a moment, irritation overtook all other emotion. She stared down at Treyam. His warm brown eyes were alight, his skin flushed with exertion. He'd dropped the weapon he'd been using – Jey's staff, which was made of fine hardwood but no match for the one Treyam loaned her with increasing frequency. *This is the problem*, she thought as she stared down, feeling the frustrated tension in her shoulders, the tightness of her jaw. *They don't take it seriously.*

If Treyam sensed her disapproval, he gave no sign. His laughter smoothed into his trademark half grin. He stretched to his full length on the smooth lawn. It was a fine day. Although the edge never seemed to leave the wind here in this high valley, today the sun was warm.

Jey found herself softening against her will. How could she blame them, really? She lifted her eyes to the jagged mountains that surrounded them, peaks reaching towards the sky like broken teeth, ringing them in on all sides. The fog lay at their base. For centuries, the Tessilari had lived with a twofold defense against reality.

In an absent gesture, Jey rubbed a hand over the inside of her elbow. Concealed there, beneath her sleeve, were the scars. There were hundreds of them – pale pricks in her skin where the needle had gone in, again and again. *I will not forget.* She made this promise to herself every day. She made it for the same reason she insisted Treyam spar with her every day. She made it because it would be so easy to let things slip. And Jey had already forgotten enough for a lifetime.

She shivered, the sweat on her brow cooling. She felt a brief stab of loneliness for Phril. He was fine, she knew. He was in one of the greenhouses, basking in the sun, stretched out on a brillbane leaf. It was too cold for the plants and tessili alike outside of the greenhouses. At first, Phril hadn't liked to be separated from her. He'd refused to stay behind. But here in the Valley of Mist, his wings grew stiff in the knife-edged air. Slowly he'd become accustomed to letting her leave him. She could feel him growing more and more complacent by the day.

On the one hand, she was glad. It had alarmed her when she'd learned other tessili could be reasonable – that they could think rationally and adjust their behavior accordingly to logic. Phril had never possessed that skill. He'd always been volatile, often behaving in ways that could easily have led to his own death, and thus Jey's as well. Seeing him change now that their lives were not in danger gave Jey hope for his sanity.

Still, she missed him a little.

Nine months, Jey had been here. She knew she'd lost her edge. Phril was going soft, Elle wasn't even trying to maintain her combat skills. The restless frustration boiled up in Jey again as she turned to stare at the mouth of the valley, where a narrow gap in the mountains stood blocked by the heavy mist.

There was a rustle of fabric as Treyam rose. He took a moment to brush the clinging grass from his sleeves. He came to Jey and stood next to her, following her gaze.

As so often happened, Jey felt a little tug of … something … when Treyam came near. He stood beside her now, his body blocking the breeze. She was aware of how close he was, how easily he could reach out and touch her.

Jey took a small step away, as she always did when she felt that tug. It wasn't that she didn't want to respond, or that she wasn't curious about where the pull might lead her. But she could see what falling in love with Lokim had done to Elle. It was another temptation Jey had to resist if she had any hope of doing what she'd promised.

The Academy still stood out there, far down in the valley of Deramor. And Jey would not let her attention be diverted until the men who had made those scars on her arm were brought to justice.

As if reading her thoughts, Treyam spoke. "Tomorrow." His voice was smooth and rich. He spoke now in a low tone, barely loud enough to hear.

"Tomorrow, at last," he said, "they will let me fulfill my promise to you."

◈

Unlike some members of the party that threaded its way through the quiet woods, Treyam had left the Valley of Mist before. He walked behind Jey, following as the girl stepped lightly over a downed branch. They were on a road – or, rather, something that had once been a road. It was broad and paved, but the paving stones had shifted and gone tilted, moss creeping up between them. In places, trees had sprouted right in the center of the walkway and shouldered the stones aside.

The road, when it had been made, had connected Deramor to the distant coast, where merchants had conducted trade with the people of the Fog Isles. Treyam knew this from his history lessons. The party of Tessilari passed other ruins as they made their way through the forest. The cracked husks of estate houses hulked over mossy ponds. The remnants of grain silos stood, split apart by trees. It had been centuries since this part of the land had housed human inhabitants. Some of the others among them paused and stared at each moldering ruin, fascinated by these remnants of a different time. Treyam didn't stare. He was used to this wood and its secrets.

Ahead of him, Jey stopped. Treyam halted as well, and those behind him did the same. They were moving single file. Jey, having the most dangerous tessila, went first.

Treyam strained to see ahead, trying to spot what had stopped Jey. He leaned to see around a tree, and understood.

Up ahead, several hundred yards off the old road, a clearing had been hacked out of the forest. It seemed a tiny space hollowed out amidst the towering trees. The house was made of timber, and a curl of smoke escaped the chimney.

"A house all the way out here." Jey spoke in a murmur, sounding amazed. Along with her words came a prod of familiar magic. Treyam accepted the rim of Jey's passive echo spell and passed it to the man in line behind him.

Their party was diminished. They'd been on the road for three days. Each day, small groups split off. The plan was to send out multiple small scouting parties, each of them bound for different settlements. Once there, they would integrate and begin to gather information about the people of Masidon.

Only Jey, Elle, Treyam, and Lokim were to continue all the way to Deramor. They would have daily contact with High Mage Agina, who would in turn report to the council. Some among the Tessilari had protested this choice, but most had conceded the point that Jey and

Elle were the only two among their number who could hope to function in court society with any sort of grace.

Treyam and Lokim were along because Lokim and Elle were inseparable, and Treyam had a way of getting what he wanted. Given his lineage, there were few among the Tessilari who would directly oppose his will. High Mage Agina was one of those few, but she had conceded to his request to go to Deramor, no doubt for reasons of her own.

What Treyam wanted, more now than ever, was to be at the center of things. And, if he was being honest, it hadn't hurt that Jey would be going to Deramor as well.

"Every month there are more people in the woods." Treyam's answer was equally quiet. Some of the older rovers spoke of a time when encountering a human anywhere beyond the outlying settlements that supplied Deramor with food was virtually unheard of.

Such was no longer the case. Deramor was full, and its inhabitants were spreading, bulging out of the valley that was the ancestral home of the Tessilari, beginning to gnaw away at the forest.

Passive echo spell in place, the group continued along the abandoned road. Two dogs lounged on the porch of the cabin, heads resting on paws. They didn't stir as the company passed.

Treyam watched Jey's pale ponytail bob and sway behind her shoulders. She walked with a fierce sort of determination. Treyam was certain he'd never met anyone as determined as Jey, not even High Mage Agina.

Dusk was falling by the time a low murmur rippled up the group, one of those behind asking for a halt. Treyam reached out and set a hand on Jey's shoulder. He wasn't sure why he did it. He knew she didn't like to be touched. She turned, ducking her shoulder out from beneath his hand.

Miat came forward, his pack large and dark on his back, broader even than the thick man's shoulders. "We go east here," he said, nodding towards a tree marked with three slashes on the trunk.

Treyam nodded and offered his hand. The two men touched palms and Miat led his small party away. Each Tessilari nodded a farewell as they passed.

Jey waited until the other group had departed. Then she shifted her pack on her shoulders and began to walk again without looking back to make sure her three friends were following.

◈

It was Lokim who led them into the shelter. It wasn't the same one he had led them to before, where he and Jey and Elle had hidden for a time before escaping to the valley. This one was in a different place, located to the east and south. It sat under a different hill, but it was nearly identical on the inside.

It was late when the four of them finally filed in out of the darkness. Jey's three companions had begun to flag shortly after sunset. They'd been making the journey in easy stages, relying on the woods for concealment. Now they'd come close to the capital. They often walked along the rims of cultivated fields. The trees, when there were any at all, were widely spaced, underbrush sparse. This was a landscape Jey and Elle knew well. Only a year ago they'd been running for their lives in these woods.

It was strange to be back in the broad, mild lands around Deramor. They'd descended steadily since leaving the Valley of Mist, leaving behind the sharp-scented pines to drop into the realm of ancient oak and ash. They had walked down and down. The air had grown steadily more warm, and more damp.

Phril had spent much of the early journey on the other side of his stitchring. The stitchring was one of the few innovations the Tessilari had created after they fled Masidon. It was a tiny portal, a loop of wire enchanted to connect to a single brillbane bush in a greenhouse. Any tessila that flew through the ring would shift across all the miles between itself and that bush in an instant.

It was an important innovation, as tessili could not live without brillbane. And a Tessilari, once joined, could not live without his tessila.

At first Phril had eschewed the cold, dark forest in favor of his bush in the warm greenhouse. Each day, though, he'd grown more interested in the journey. Now he was with Jey, and he was delighted. The air in this valley was warm and rich with summer. He could fly without getting a chill. His high spirits filtered back to Jey as he darted through the hatch ahead of her and disappeared into the darkness.

Not long ago, Jey would have worried about him flying off on his own like that, fearing the shelter might not have been well sealed. There could be cats or bats or territorial birds lurking in the darkness. His body being only about the length of her thumb, for a long time, Jey had considered Phril vulnerable.

That was before he'd learned to shift. Now Phril was capable of expanding to the size of a large dog. At that size, with sharp talons, wings, and a jaw full of teeth, he was formidable.

Still, Jey looked after her tessili, unable to keep from worrying. The first few times Phril had shifted, he'd made himself as large as a horse. But in the months since their arrival at the Valley of Mists, he'd never been able to repeat that feat. Treyam's theory was the absence of mortal danger made him less inclined to push his limits. But Jey, knowing temperance was the least pronounced of all Phril's traits, wasn't so sure.

Jey walked to the center of the room as Treyam followed, holding aloft a spherical spell that glowed in his palm. It was an passive luminance spell, Jey knew, but it was one she'd never been particularly good at. She also wasn't great at the active ignition spell Lokim cast a few moments later after he'd carried an armful of logs to the fire ring. It seemed Jey's talents, no matter how hard she tried to shift them, continued to lie in one direction. If it didn't involve maiming or killing, she wasn't good at it.

As the fire began to dance, Jey set her pack down on one of the sleeping stones. As the fire caught and bloomed, a low rippling light spread along the bas relief carvings that adorned the walls. To her eye, this chamber seemed an exact copy of the one they'd stayed in before, complete with withered brillbane bushes and a thick coat of gritty dust on the floor. These shelters had been created by the Tessilari to keep their people safe in the eventuality the diods reached the capital. That hadn't happened. Instead, after that war, the people of Masidon had turned on the Tessilari, fearing the very magic that had saved their lives.

Taken by surprise, already weakened by the long war, and facing weapons they themselves had crafted so men without magics could stand against the diods, the Tessilari had fallen. Most had died fighting. Some few had fled. Others had been captured and taken to the academy, where they'd been forced to create the school that had produced Jey and Elle.

With the fire lit, Lokim settled down to skin the rabbits his tessila, Bliz, had caught for dinner. The orange tessila was a stealthy, effective hunter, and caught twice as many rabbits as the rest of the tessili combined. Phril himself was not much skilled at hunting. He was ferocious if attacked, but strategy was not his forte.

Jey sighed, gazing in blank fatigue at the dancing murals that were coming to life around the edges of the room. She felt so limited sometimes. Elle had learned dozens of new spells during their time in the valley. Treyam was a versatile caster with a seemingly endless ability to improvise and adapt his magic on the fly.

Jey was only good at one thing. And it was something she loathed.

Her mouth tightened as Phril remerged from the darkness, coming in for a quick landing to cling to the collar of her leather vest. Looking down, she ran her finger along the fine edge of his skull. Her thoughts drifted towards the academy. At least her talents would still have use for a short while. There were some people in the world yet who deserved to die.

She heard the light creak of leather and turned to see Elle setting her pack down by another sleeping stone. She noticed Jey watching and her mouth bent in a wan smile. "I'm out of shape," she said, rubbing her shoulders where the pack's straps had chafed. "I'm rubbed raw, and I'll need to wear a wide-necked gown within a few days. If they're still in style, that is."

Jey glanced towards the fire. Treyam had joined Lokim, but the two men weren't talking. They crouched on either side of the fire, working on the rabbits in brittle silence. Jey still didn't know what had happened between the two of them that caused such tension. When she asked Treyam, he dodged the question. When she asked Lokim, he either went stiff and silent or simply walked away.

"Treyam could heal the chafing," Jey said. Treyam had a particular gift for healing. As she spoke, she seemed to feel a bloom of remembered heat in her own calf where she still bore the faintest of scars to remind her of the vicious puncture Nylan's knife had left in her leg. Treyam had healed her, clamping his firm hands over the torn muscle and making it whole. Moments later, he'd healed Lokim's cracked skull. But Jey could barely manage to smooth over her own blisters.

Elle's face flushed in the low light at her friend's suggestion. "Oh, I can heal them myself," she said. "I'm just being a wimp." Then she gave a light, uncomfortable laugh, and drifted away towards the fire.

# CHAPTER 2

The stone set above the northern entry hatch began to glow. Jey looked up from her work, squinting. It was a bright, cloudless day. The sunstone of the ceiling let the brilliant light spill down unchecked.

Jey was sharpening her knives. She'd neglected her weapons somewhat these last months. In the Valley of Mist, there was no need to hunt. The Tessilari kept herds of domesticated goats that thrived on the sparse grasses of the high meadows and flocks of lean game hens that pecked for seeds among the pine trees. While some of the ingenious greenhouses were devoted to the brillbane that supported the tessili, others were full of cultivated plants that produced an impressive variety of plump fruits and colorful vegetables.

Jey and Elle had both been interviewed and assessed upon their arrival in the valley. Elle had been put to work in the clinic, where her soft voice and gentle hands were appreciated. She was taught any number of practical spells that might ease a sick child or a woman in labor.

Jey, on the other hand, had been assigned an axe and sent to a barren camp where downed trees were hauled to be chopped into firewood. Day after day, she'd split logs and watched the quick clouds cross the sky, waiting to be summoned by the council, fearing she'd made a mistake in trusting Treyam.

Treyam, later, had assured her the assignment was not a veiled insult or a punishment of any kind. "Many here are too old or too young for heavy work," he'd said. "And our numbers are fewer each season. You're a valuable resource."

Today, Jey had made a systematic review of her weapon's belt. She'd considered the callouses on her palms as she rubbed oil into the grips of her knives. She'd healed a ragged hangnail that had left the tip of one finger tender. A warrior had to take care of her hands.

The sunlight in the chamber was so bright Jey wouldn't have seen the stone above the hatch begin to glow if she hadn't been watching for it. As soon as she saw the telltale light, she stood, setting her whetstone aside and settling her knife into her palm. She waited, watching the dim hallway that led into the shelter from the hatch. Phril, who'd already begun to grow bored with the chamber, flew over to loop in lazy circles around her head.

Footsteps sounded in the hall. A woman appeared, walking out of the shadows. For a moment, Jey could only stare.

The woman wore a fine gown, rich without being ornate, marred only slightly by the few damp areas along the bottom of the skirts that indicated she'd been walking through a forest rather than along a cobbled street.

As she passed out of the hatch and continued towards Jey, the familiar set of her shoulders and tilt of her jaw made Jey's head spin.

Because nothing else about Elle was recognizable.

Her friend continued a few more paces into the room, then stopped. Her expression was a mingled blend of self-satisfaction and annoyance. She directed her strangely light eyes at the weapon Jey held at ready. "I take it the disguise is working, then?"

Even her voice was different. Jey, flushing, shoved the knife back into its sheath. Phril, fascinated, swept towards Elle and danced a circle around her body.

She was transformed, but the changes were subtle. Her forehead was a little too high, her nose a little too long. Her eyes were a different color, set too close. Her waist was a little too thick, her hair two shades too light.

It all combined to make Jey's oldest friend into a stranger.

When Jey's only response was to stare, Elle laughed and glanced around the bright, expansive room. "Where's Lokim?"

Jey managed to tear her eyes away. Shai, who'd been hiding at the base of Elle's braid, stuck his spiked head out and hissed at Phril, who hissed back but looped away, his red wings brilliant in the sunlight. "Still out gathering. So is Treyam." Jey herself had downed a large goose early in the day and returned to clean the carcass and prepare the meat, setting most of it in the smoke room to cure. They wanted to stockpile as much food as possible. Fortunately, this place was equipped to help with the work of keeping many people sheltered and fed for long periods of time.

Elle looked disappointed. She gazed down at her muddied skirt, sighed, and her face seemed to smear. The magic fell away from her in slow loops. Jey blinked. Her friend was herself again. "That's amazing," Jey said.

Elle grimaced, heading towards the pegs on the wall where she'd hung her leathers. "Hardly," she said. "It's just a dozen passive distortion spells, held on different parts of my body. It's way less work than one big passive echo spell. I think, with practice, I'll be able to hold them for hours at a time."

Jey walked over to the fire, stirred up the coals, and dropped on a log or two. They didn't need the warmth, but somehow this central fire powered the entire chamber. It heated the pool in the back that was for bathing and caused the smoke room to grow hot and fill with smoke. The sheer complexity of the magics, the sophisticated understanding of the principles of enchantment that would have been required to create such a place, made Jey's head spin.

Across the room, Elle began to work her way out of her fine gown. Shai flew to the lacing at her back and pulled on the tie until it came free and Elle could continue with her fingers. "I found a house," Elle said in a cheery voice as she worked. "It's a good price. The family selling it seems to have left the city rather suddenly. It's well positioned on High Street. I can set up there, and go about introducing myself to old friends." She laughed.

While Jey had been primarily used as an assassin during her years at Tessili Academy, Elle had been something subtler. She'd had an entire false persona and had been sent into Deramor on a regular basis to use her gifts at passive persuasion to ensure certain people behaved and thought in certain ways. Because of this past, Elle felt at home in Masidon's capital. She was adept when it came to the intrigue of the court. Their plan was to set her up in town and establish her there under a new identity. She would gather intelligence and be poised to use her talents to influence important people when needed.

Jey poked at the fire again, chewing on her lip. It was all going to take so *long*. It would be months before Elle was established, even longer before she had a true grasp of the current political environment, and longer still before they could take what she learned and use it to somehow bring down the academy.

"The price hardly matters." Jey spoke under her breath, but her friend heard, and frowned. Elle didn't like to be reminded her funds had all been stolen. She sniffed, hung up her dress, and began to pull her leathers on over her underclothes.

Jey set the stick she'd been using to poke the fire aside, hearing the meanness of the comment. "I'm sorry, Elle." She spoke with sincerity, trying to rally. "You were amazing today. This would never work without you."

Elle tied her breeches into place, giving Jey a small smile over her shoulder. But when she turned, her eyes were sad. She walked over to the fire and set a hand on her friend's arm. "I want to get those girls out of the academy as badly as you," she said. "But you know the risk. Right now, we lose one or two a year. If we mess this up, they could all be murdered."

As awful as they were, the words were true. Still, Jey had a hard time accepting them. It was a brutal kind of equation. The Tessilari were slow. They'd survived all this time by hiding. If they were going to reveal themselves now, they had to make sure to do it the right way.

Jey looked up at the bright ceiling, her eyes suddenly hot. "It's almost time for graduation," she said.

Elle's hand fell to her side. She walked back to where her boots lay and stepped into one. She spoke in a sad, low voice. "I know."

◈

Professor Liam walked through the dim corridors of the faculty compound, making his quiet way towards his bedchamber. Around him, most of the large windows were open, letting in the fine night breeze. It was late, nearing midnight, and Liam did not carry a candle. He'd been in the library, as he often was these nights, filling his head with useless knowledge.

The truth was, Professor Liam didn't sleep well these days. Ever since that night when the seniors Jey and Elle had escaped, the atmosphere in Tessili Academy had been tense. Their friend Kae, Liam knew now, had not been as fortunate. The faculty had all been summoned to a meeting hall the next morning. Kae's body had been on display there, arranged next to the crushed remains of her tessila.

Liam and the other professors had been addressed by the dean himself. This tragedy, the man had said, had come about due to negligence on the part of the faculty. Everyone knew contact with magics unhinged the human mind, stripped away the moral compass, and left behind a monster in human form. That was why most children who showed any aptitude for spellwork were humanely put out of their misery before they could cause any harm. This was why no tessili were allowed to exist outside the academy walls.

Tessili Academy, the dean had gone on, was a special place – a haven for young girls, a place they could learn and grow and have a life they would otherwise have been denied. But magics were crafty. The forces these girls manipulated were evil and tireless. Corruption could sneak past the defenses the academy kept in place. When that happened, tragedy was the result.

He'd gestured at the dead girl, his face a false mask of sorrow. Liam had stared at Kae's unmarred face, remembering all the times she'd sat in his classroom, her tessila on a holdstone, struggling to learn despite all the blocks in her mind and the drugged state of amnesia in which she passed her days.

Everyone in Masidon knew about magic, but it was a subject never discussed. Children sometimes disappeared suddenly, without explanation. When this happened, no one said anything. Parents mourned behind closed doors. Neighbors looked the other way. When Liam had been a boy, it had happened to a girl on his street.

But it wasn't only children. Sometimes rumors would start to fly about a particular adult – strange, inexplicable stories that piled up little by little. Then, without exception, that person would die. It was invariably a peaceful passing during the night blamed on a failure of the heart, or a spasm in the brain. People mourned, feeling secretly relieved it had not happened in their family. Liam didn't know anything for certain, but he had a theory about what caused those deaths.

He reached the end of the silent hall and opened the door to his bedchamber. His was a generous room with polished floors and large windows. Every room in the faculty compound was ornate, as if the men who lived here could be fooled into forgetting they were prisoners. Liam's large bed was tucked against the far wall. His desk stood before the open windows.

Liam took one step into the room, then froze.

There was someone sitting at his desk.

For a moment, Liam felt a kind of dull, fatalistic terror. *They have found me out at last.* The thought came with a strange sense of relief. Ever since Jey and Elle had fled, Liam had waited, convinced some bit of evidence would come to light and reveal his role in what had happened.

A year and a quarter had passed since the night Liam had stood at his window and watched two girls cross the bridge. He'd heard a report they'd been killed, but Liam was skeptical. Unlike with Kae, no bodies had been presented to the faculty.

And the academy had changed. The students were more closely monitored now. He'd been unable, this year, to make any progress with the current seniors. So, in his frustration, Liam had turned to the library. The collection of books in the faculty compound was truly amazing. It was a disorganized mass of every kind of book on magic. He'd read and read. And while he'd learned many interesting things, he'd come up with nothing that could help either the students or himself.

Still, Liam searched. He couldn't shake the feeling of building pressure – like a late summer storm gathering just beyond the horizon. The academy was tense, the orderlies vigilant. Only a week ago a student had vanished – not a junior or senior, but an initiate only recently introduced to spellwork. It wasn't unheard of for a young student to disappear, but it hadn't happened in a long time.

Then, three days later, Liam had read a small announcement on the faculty board stating High Handler Nylan had retired.

Liam could only guess at the implications. He knew very little about what the girls did on their opportunities. He was a cog in this great machine, only marginally more free than the girls he taught. While his own life was not in jeopardy on a daily basis, he too, one day, would reach the end of his time here. He'd attended retirement parties for other faculty members, seen the slick look of fear in the faces of the professors who'd grown too old to continue their work. Liam didn't believe they left this place for a peaceful decline any more than he believed seniors graduated and went on to live full, happy lives in the outside world.

As Liam stood frozen in his doorway, the form in his chair unfolded. He didn't know who he'd expected, but it wasn't this slender girl. As she stood, a ray of moonlight fell across her back, illuminating her light hair. "Jey?" He spoke the word in a low, hope-filled whisper.

She smiled. Liam turned quickly to close the door. His heart was suddenly pounding, his mind scrambling. "You're alive." He made sure the latch was fastened. Then he turned, crossing the room to go to her, stopping when he was close enough to see her dark eyes. "Where's Elle?" He glanced around the room as if he might find her standing in a corner.

"Safe," Jey said. "But I don't have much time. You must listen."

And then she told him everything.

◈

Nylan jerked the leash. The grubby girl on the other end stumbled to a stop. She didn't look at Nylan, but sank to the ground in dull exhaustion.

Nylan could smell the girl. She bore the musty scent of unwashed human, overlaid with a tang of blood and rot. He could smell himself as well. They were both filthy and exhausted. If they'd had much further to go, they might not have made it.

He stood for a moment in the thick forest, all his weight resting on his good leg. His bad knee was alive with pain. Today his limp had become so severe he'd nearly fallen a few times.

Still, Nylan felt only an overpowering swell of satisfaction as he stood in the small clearing and stared at the rock face before him. The stone was rough and gray, unremarkable except for the rune chiseled at eye-level, its edges as sharp and distinct as if it had been carved the day before.

At last, Nylan was here. Although the place he now stood was less than half a day's travel from the city of Deramor, it had taken him quite some time to pinpoint the spot. He had dragged the girl back and forth in sweeps for days. But his journey was over. He leaned on the strange stone cane he carried, the surface of which was carved with similar runes and signs, and a sense of triumph built in his chest. Success was his. He had achieved the goal he'd set out to accomplish so long ago.

It hadn't been easy. All the forces of the world had seemed to work against him. Nylan had sacrificed much to get here. He'd been stripped of his identity and his freedom alike when he'd been made a handler at the academy. Then it had been years of careful toil, calculated steps, and his first murder to allow him to achieve the position of High Handler at such a young age.

From there, he'd thought it would be easy. With the seniors at his disposal, he'd set to work orchestrating the slow process of shifting the opinions of a populace. His strategy had been simple. Every time an order came from the Council to send a senior on an opportunity, Nylan had deployed the students as bidden, but also added an extra task of his own. It had worked beautifully for several years. He'd been on task, able to truthfully report he was on course to achieve what he'd promised.

But the number of students at the academy was dwindling. Nylan had fewer seniors to work with every year. Worse, the more he used them, the more unstable they seemed to become.

Finally, disaster struck. Three seniors had escaped. Nylan had nearly lost his position and his life alike. He'd begged for a chance to recover the seniors, and it had been granted. He'd regained some stature when he'd reported the threat neutralized. That lie had been easy enough to sell. It only took threatening the two students who'd been with him that day and using them to convince several guards and orderlies they'd seen the escapees die. The bodies of the girls and their little monsters, he'd explained, had fallen into the river.

Nylan had been restored to his position, but his task, the task he'd gone to the academy to carry out in the first place, was in danger of failing. And his long-time employer, the High Priest of Masidon, also Nylan's father, was not happy. The critical vote was only a few weeks away. Nylan had been unable to deploy seniors to sway several key members of the council.

Nylan and his father had long ago hatched the plan Nylan had worked tirelessly to achieve for the majority of his life. Using the Academy and its secret magical forces the church kept hidden from the world, Nylan had agreed to keep his own existence a secret, and also help the High Priest establish the House of Merchants and win appointment to its head, giving him more power in Masidon than either the King or the Queen. In return, the High Priest would give Nylan the map to the mythical grotto where the Tessilari had hidden their riches before they'd fallen.

The agreement had always seemed fair enough to Nylan. But as his plan fell apart piece by piece, Nylan realized he needed a different way of getting what he wanted. Fortunately, he'd always been a quick thinker with an ability to conceive of alternative solutions.

With failure imminent, Nylan decided not to wait. In retrospect, he was a little shocked it had taken him so long to realize how strong a hand he held. When he understood the vote might not be cast in his father's favor, he sent a senior to the High Priest's mansion. She returned with the document Nylan now clutched in his free hand: the map Nylan had devoted his life to possessing.

Nylan looked down at it now, a strange thrill shooting through his chest. It was only a copy, but whomever had made the duplicate had taken pains to reproduce the damage the original had sustained. Much of the thick paper was blank. There had once been a headline, but only the letters ILARI remained towards the right edge. A few more incomplete words had been faithfully reproduced as well.

Fortunately, what had been lost appeared not to be very important. The center of the scroll was intact. A sentence started out of blankness "… vault can only be opened by one of the Tessilari."

Below was a map, an illustration of the rune that would mark its location, and a description of the spell that would be needed to open the stone.

It was enough.

Nylan jerked the leash again. The girl moaned, but did not rise. He lifted the rope he wore around his own neck. At its end hung a small cage. A tessila lay inside the cage, weighed down by one of the heavy harnesses the academy had devised to keep the ridiculous creatures from killing themselves when separated from their students. The tessila in the cage was in even worse shape than the girl. It had refused to eat since being taken captive. While Nylan had worked around this by forcing a brillbane solution down its throat with a syringe, the beast was all but comatose. It seemed to be willfully imposing death upon its body.

He raised the cage, his threat implicit, and the girl struggled upright with another moan. "The spell," Nylan said, handing her the page.

He'd made the girl prove she could understand and execute the spell before he'd kidnapped her. She'd been a promising initiate, capable of casting spells but young enough to be less dangerous than the juniors and seniors. Still, Nylan felt his chest constrict with fear as she stumbled towards the rune. He limped after, holding her leash, leaning heavily on his weapon.

The girl reached the stone and set her hands on the rune. She glanced over her shoulder at him, touching a depression in the stone that had been carved out to form a small ledge. "My tessila needs to sit here, outside of the cage. He has to touch the stone."

Her voice was a small, broken thing. Nylan looped the end of the leash about his wrist so he could work the catch on the cage and lift the weighted creature out. He set it on the ledge, making sure to keep his body between it and the girl.

The girl stared at the little beast with a kind of desperate hunger. He gave the leash another jerk to remind her of her task. Her neck under the collar was bloody. Yellow puss had soaked into the collar of her dress. He could smell the infection. But it didn't matter. As soon as she opened this vault for him, he would kill her creature, which would mean she would die as well.

The girl dropped her eyes to the rune.

It happened very quickly, then. She did nothing that he could see, made no noise or gesture. But the rune began to glow. A moment later, a fine crack appeared in the cliff face. A rumble started deep within the rock. A slab slid aside, revealing a hidden chamber.

Nylan felt a swell of triumph, a giddy rush of satisfaction that coursed through him like a drug. For a moment he forgot his shattered knee, his long years of toil, his lost youth.

The plan, of course, had been for the High Priest and his bastard son to open this door together. It was rumored the riches and artifacts within were powerful and sophisticated, that they would give a man the gifts of a god. This was even better. Nylan wouldn't have to share.

But first things first. Nylan must neutralize the last remaining threat. He lifted his hand towards the half dead tessila, intending to end its pitiful life.

Nylan's hand was raised, fingers only a bare inch from the ledge where the tessila lay, when a streak of light shot out of the dark space beyond the door. It was a strange light, murky and purple, and somehow cold. It hit Nylan in the chest. He discovered with surprise he could not longer move. For a moment, he stared into the darkness, seeing nothing, frozen in place. Then he saw a shift, and a glow, more purple light illuminating a hunched, spectral form.

Nylan was dimly aware of the tessila inching its slow way to edge of the ledge, and falling. It tumbled through the air, wings limp. The girl darted forward, catching it before it hit the ground. She jerked against the collar then, throwing the entire weight of her small body against the leash. Nylan, immobile, felt the rope unloop from around his wrist and fall free. Before he could register this or react in any way, the girl scurried away into the trees.

Nylan had eyes only for the creature that hunched in the purple shadows. It moved towards him, resolving out of darkness. The purple beam of light that had hit him and frozen him, he could now see, originated from a withered, claw-like hand. A thought erupted in his mind – a thought that was in his head but somehow not his. The mind it seemed to come from was an ancient, craggy thing. *Hungy hungry hungry need eat need servant wait use this one hungry.*

Fear flowed though Nylan. It came with the sick realization that he had been wrong. Frantically, he tried to recall the partial words that had been on the scroll. He remembered, belatedly, seeing the letters "iod" and "ainment."

Understanding crystalized in Nylan's mind, too late to do him any good. *Diod.* Two of something.

The histories said the Tessilari had faced an army. The thoughts that now seeped into Nylan's head told him otherwise.

There had been only two diods. The Tessilari had destroyed one, breaking their own strength in the process. The other diod, they had trapped here.

And Nylan had just set it free.

Jey hopped the creek that ran through the quiet woods, almost smiling at the familiar sounds of the babbling water. She felt a strange swell of nostalgia. The route she was following was a familiar one. How many times had she walked this way, carrying a bundle of brillbane and listening for sounds of pursuit?

She now remembered the days she and Elle had lived at the cheesery to hide from the academy with a kind of quiet wonder. They'd been terrified, hunted, and alone. They'd also been completely naïve. It seemed to Jey she'd been a different person then.

Now, the dawn was just beginning to fade the night from the sky. Jey was returning from her second visit to Professor Liam. She knew she couldn't go to him too often. It was hard to resist the pull, though. He'd told her the academy had declared Jey and Elle dead, Nylan was retired, and all the efforts of the orderlies, guards, and handlers were focused inward, on the current students. This meant it was child's play for Jey to slip in and out of the faculty compound undetected.

It had been a relief to find Professor Liam unharmed, to know that he hadn't suffered for what he'd done to help them. As Jey walked around the base of old, cracked oak, she thought of two other people who might have been declared guilty by association.

She didn't know what had become of Holdam and Biala – the older couple who she and Elle had lived with at their cheesery. The night Lokim had finally convinced them to flee, Elle had nearly exhausted herself altering Holdam and Biala's memories. Only moments later, the academy's agents had arrived. The girls had never had an opportunity to go back and see if the couple had survived.

Jey's footfalls began to land a little faster. The forest around her thinned. At last, she stepped onto a lane. In the distance, she saw an orchard. Across the road from the fruit trees stood an archway, the familiar gates flung open.

From here, nothing looked any different. Jey drew her cloak in more tightly, ready to cast a passive echo spell should encounter some early tradesman on the road. She wouldn't speak to anyone, she promised herself. She would just look in to see if Holdam and Biala were safe.

Walking quickly now, Jey reached the archway and ducked through. The yard opened around her. Ahead lay the house, its painted wooden door colorless in the tentative dawn light. The fresh scent of clover filled the air. Around back, she knew, stood the small room she and Elle had lived in, the cheesery itself, and the animal pens.

Jey paused in the yard, suddenly uncertain. It was too early even for Holdam to be stirring. He'd be asleep, which meant she'd need to break into his house and creep into his bedroom to learn anything. She chewed her lip for a moment, standing in the quiet yard. A light breeze stirred her hair. She felt suddenly very alone. Phril was dozing on his brillbane bush far away, though he could return to her at any time. The silver stitchring was a cool presence against the skin of her chest.

Jey was on the verge of changing her mind, of turning to go, when a sudden light flared in the dim dawn. It came not from the front windows, but from the kitchen at the back of the house. Jey could see the light reflected on the pale wall that encircled the cheesery. Encouraged, she drew up to the house.

She'd been expecting to see Biala, hair tied back in a gray braid, stooping over the oven as she stirred up the fire. What she actually saw sent a ripple of shock and confusion through her. The emotion was so forceful, Phril woke up in a heartbeat and launched himself off his bush. He burst through the stitchring and tangled in Jey's shirt, where he clawed and hissed. Jey's vision darkened slightly and her mind felt momentarily cloudy as the working of the spell on the stitchring drew the

considerable pull of energy it required. She blinked, freed
Phril, and tried to convince herself she hadn't seen what
she thought she'd seen. She looked through the window
again.

But the girl was still there, seated on a stool in
Holdam and Biala's kitchen. She was young and slight,
probably not yet 10. And she wore the unmistakable blue
gown of an initiate of Tessili Academy.

Holdam and Biala were there as well. Biala wore a
faded house-coat. Holdam was fully dressed, but his
cheeks were rough with stubble. There were visible tear
tracks on Biala's face, and Holdam looked both angry
and scared.

Phril hissed at the sight of the girl. He stalked down
Jey's arm to draw closer to the window. Then he went
still as Jey noticed where the attention of all three people
was directed.

A tessila lay on the table in an inert heap. It was
immobile in a way that was entirely unnatural for one of
the temperamental creatures. Jey looked more critically
at the girl, this time noting that her dress was filthy and
ragged, the skirts torn to ribbons. Her hair was more of a
tangle than a braid. And Jey also saw how the girl sagged
on her stool. Her eyes, blank and glazed over, were fixed
on her inert tessila.

# CHAPTER 3

Jey had no illusions as to how well her decision was going to go over with the Tessilari. She hadn't technically even been authorized to visit Professor Liam. Her place among the Tessilari was not a comfortable one. For nine months she'd been pushing them to do something about the academy, all the while fearing she'd given away too much freedom for the security of the hidden valley. Now that she was back out in the world, being able to take action without first asking permission felt liberating.

Still, she was walking a fine line. She hadn't been forbidden to visit Liam, but she didn't doubt the Tessilari would issue such an order if they learned of her late-night activities. She could only imagine they'd be even less happy if she revealed herself to two citizens of Masidon.

But the girl was in bad shape. The tessila seemed even worse. The strained looks on Holdam and Biala's faces showed that they did not know how to help. How could they?

Jey made her decision, and began to move. Consequences be damned, she was here, and she was going to help. She crept around the side of the house to the back and tried the latch on the door that led into the kitchen from the yard. It turned easily.

Jey pushed, and stepped inside.

Holdam and Biala both jumped and spun as the latch clicked. Biala's face blanched as Jey stepped in and closed the door behind her. Holdam's reaction was more surprising. He glanced about the room, darted to the side, and grabbed a cleaver from its hook on the wall. He placed himself squarely between Jey and the girl on the stool, his plain, solid face a sudden mask of rage. He spoke, his normally friendly voice grating out in low a growl. "We'll not be giving her up again."

Jey blinked, surprised into stillness. Phril bridled at the threat, rearing back onto his hind legs and flaring his wings. Only Jey's very firm desire that he not leave her person kept the small creature from flinging himself onto Holdam in a fury. He had grown a little more tractable during their months with the tessilari. A little.

Holdam's eyes shifted from Jey's face to Phril, and it was his turn to go silent with surprise. How Jey wished Elle was here right now. Elle had a way of talking, of smoothing over awkward moments, of putting everyone at ease.

As Jey wondered at the anger in Holdam's face and the fear in Biala's, she realized her mistake. She was wearing the leathers she'd stolen from the academy. They were comfortable and practical, durable and resilient. But if Holdam and Biala had been interrogated by a student after Jey and Elle had left the cheesery, they would doubtless recognize the outfit and associate it with whatever they had suffered that night.

Jey spoke in a low tone she hoped was soothing. "I'm not what you think I am."

Biala spoke next. Her jaw firmed up, and she moved around the table to place her soft, round body between Jey and the girl on the stool, clutching a paring knife. The idea that these two gentle people would react to her presence this way was almost more painful than if they'd actually stabbed her. Biala didn't address Jey, but spoke to her husband. "This is the one they warned us about," she said. "Light hair, dark eyes, red tessila."

Jey could only guess the experience this couple must have been through after Jey and Elle had fled. Since Elle had modified their memories, they would have forgotten the months of knowing the two girls, of working alongside them in the cheesery. They doubtless would have been told terrible stories and made to promise to report back to the academy if they ever saw Jey or Elle. So this part of their reaction was no surprise.

What Jey couldn't figure out was the girl. How had she escaped? And why was she here?

Jey thought back, and lit on a particular memory. It had happened shortly after Jey and Elle had installed themselves at the cheesery. They hadn't yet realized, then, how alone they were in this world. They didn't know wild brillbane had been eradicated, tessili exterminated.

One afternoon, Elle had asked innocently why there didn't seem to be any tessili about. Holdam had gone pale and defensive, spluttering that no one in his family had any love for magics.

Now, a few things clicked in Jey's mind. She made a tenuous connection, and took a risk. She needed a way to slice through the fear and defensiveness if she was going to help the girl.

She spoke, injecting her voice with confidence. "Your granddaughter will die if her tessila is not attended to very soon. I can help, but you have to trust me."

◈

It was midday by the time Jey returned to the shelter. She should have been exhausted. She hadn't slept since the short nap she'd taken the previous afternoon. She'd spent all night talking to Liam, and all morning trying to bring a tessila back from the dead.

As she approached the entry hatch, however, Jey felt full of a kind frantic energy, and also a strange sort of joy. Holdam and Biala walked a few steps behind her, the sleeping child cradled in her grandfather's arms. The girl's tessila was with Phril on the other side of the stitchring.

For once, Jey had helped. She'd done something useful that didn't involve killing, though it had been a very close call.

It was the girl's collapse that had broken the stalemate. After Jey had spoken, the child had simply gone slack, slumping off her stool to be caught by her grandfather. His cleaver had fallen to the stone floor with a ringing clang. Jey had rushed across the room, ignoring the knife Biala threatened her with. She'd reached out to scoop the tessila into her hands. The creature had felt cold and limp, but had still carried a spark of life.

Healing had never been Jey's strength, but the animal was more exhausted and malnourished than harmed. She'd bolstered him with a few active vitality spells and sent him through the stitchring with Phril. Then had come the harder part – convincing Holdam and Biala to carry their unconscious granddaughter out into the woods.

Jey worked the spell on the entry hatch. She felt a little thrill of energy, the clarity that always came to her right before a fight. The Tessilari would all be very, very angry. At first, anyway. But when they understood, she hoped they would forgive her.

The hidden hatch in the hillside flashed and opened inwards. Behind her, Holdam gave a little gasp of surprise. Jey did not look back. Instead, she walked straight into what had been a slab of blank stone a moment before. There was a pause, then the heavy tread of Holdam's boots told her he was following.

Jey had expected to find her friends worried, perhaps even angry. She'd particularly anticipated Elle's annoyance. But when she entered the shelter, she looked for Elle in vain. Lokim was on the far side of the room, stripped to the waist, clearing away dead brillbane bushes with a spade. Treyam was by the fire, holding a leather tablet and a scribis. Back in the Valley of Mist, Jey knew, an identical tablet would be receiving the imprint of his marks, and a diligent scribe would even now be transcribing the message to be delivered to its recipient. This was how the Tessilari communicated over distances.

Treyam looked up when Jey entered. Jey saw some worry lines smooth out of his face. He stood, throwing his long coat back and setting the scribis aside. "Jey," he said. "You shouldn't stay away so long. Elle was beside herself this morning. She almost didn't go through with the purchase."

Jey bit her lip, feeling guilty. She'd forgotten Elle would be occupied this morning, finalizing the acquisition of the townhouse that was a critical part of her identity.

"I'm sorry," Jey managed to murmur as Treyam's amber eyes left Jey and flew to the three people who had just followed her into the shelter.

The rhythmic thudding of Lokim's spade stilled. Behind Holdam and Biala, the entry hatch hissed shut. Holdam jumped at the sound, and looked back at the sealed exit.

"Treyam," Jey said, "something has happened." Then she repeated the story Holdam and Biala had told her, which their sobbing granddaughter had imparted to them in the middle of the night when she'd arrived, filthy and half dead, at the cheesery door.

By the time Jey was finished, the mood in the shelter had shifted. Lokim had set aside his spade, donned his shirt, and joined them by the fire. The girl was asleep on one of the warm sleeping stones. Holdam and Biala, looking gray and tired, were seated with the others by the fire. Jey had told the story, with Holdam and Biala adding their voices here and there. Jey couldn't understand what any of it might mean. Nylan kidnapping a child, forcing her to open a sealed stone with a spell devised by the Tessilari. Then the purple light, the child's escape, and the screams she'd heard as she'd fled.

Treyam and Lokim had gone very still as they'd listened. Now, Treyam looked at the cheese maker and his wife, the little sly grin that normally hovered around the edges of his lips was entirely absent. He said in a serious tone, "You are certain she said the light was purple?"

Both Holdam and Biala nodded in vigorous assent. "She said purple," Biala said, "and dark, somehow, even though it was light."

Treyam closed his eyes for a moment, then opened them again. "We need to get Elle back here immediately," he said, "and we need to tell the Tessilari what has happened. If what the child says is true, this changes everything."

# TESSILI REVENGE

◈

The streets of Deramor were quiet and nearly empty, most of the day's activity spent. A half-moon hung behind low clouds, hovering like a luminous ghost. Treyam walked at a steady pace, his stride a little shorter than it would have been, had he been alone. Elle, hampered as she was by her heavy skirts, wasn't moving as quickly as usual.

Treyam held his half of the passive echo spell in place without difficulty, all the while acutely aware of the invisible seam in the spell where his magic knit into Jey's. As always, her spell was solid and sure, the energy of her mind steady and firm. He glanced to the side, watching her slender form as she stalked along the street on the other side of Lokim and Elle.

The night was warm, with a heavy breeze blowing in from the south. It had been just over twenty-four hours since news of the diod's release had reached them. In that time, they'd been in near constant communication with the leaders of the Tessilari. Everyone had agreed, for once, that it was time to act. Any sort of delay could bring about catastrophic consequences to the people of Masidon and the Tessilari alike.

The time for hiding was over.

Treyam couldn't help but feel a stir of anticipation as they walked. It was unequivocally bad news, of course, that the diod was free. The children in the Valley of Mist practically grew up on stories of the Two Wars. It had taken all the considerable strength of the ancient Tessilari to contain the diods when the two monsters had come out of the mountains without warning and fallen upon what had been a peaceful, thriving country.

Logically, Treyam should be scared. What hope had the tattered, marginalized remains of his people of standing against the creature that had taken down the strongest mages in history? But while Treyam as a boy had listened to the stories with terror and awe, he now couldn't help but wonder if the Tessilari of old had grown complacent, lulled into ease by centuries of peace and plenty.

The Tessilari may be few now, and weaker, but they had two things. First, they were fighting for their very existence. Second, they had information. The story of how the first diod had been defeated had been made into a ballad, which was sung at every solstice celebration.

Surely, this was their moment. Without the Tessilari, the people of Masidon were more helpless than newly hatched tessili. They had no hope of standing against a creature of such might and magic as a diod. The Tessilari would help. In doing so, they would regain the trust and respect of Masidon.

At least, this was what Treyam hoped. It was easy to see it all play out in his head as he walked with the others along the wide, cobbled streets, making their way ever deeper into the heart of the city.

There were guards stationed at the entryway to the administrative city, but the gates were open. Jey walked right through, followed by Lokim, Elle, and finally Treyam. The guards never so much as glanced over. Once they were a block away from the gatehouse, Lokim moved into the lead. Although Treyam had never approved of Lokim's rash decision to leave the valley against the will of the council, it was turning out the year the young man had spent in the capital had yielded a lot of useful information.

Lokim had spent his time in Masidon before he'd met Elle and Jey learning about the government and spying on secret meetings. He knew the daily, aboveground rhythm of the three houses, and also the more clandestine activities of their heads. Once he'd discovered the academy, he'd applied himself to understanding what it was. He'd grown to believe that only the High Priest and his inner council, of all the people in Masidon, knew of the academy's existence.

Tonight, according to Lokim, the King and Queen would be together. This meeting happened on a weekly basis. It was not exactly a secret event, but it was a private one. Various officials and nobles were invited, but as far as Lokim knew, the High Priest had never been on that list.

It was, they'd all decided, their best chance at delivering the information they wanted to pass to the King and Queen without interference. Showing up at such an event uninvited and unannounced would certainly make an impression. They would use surprise and fear to make their offer more attractive. They would be generous, but firm. Forgiving, but steady. They would offer to help, but for a price.

The group of four walked on, the streets so wide two carriages could pass abreast with room for pedestrians on either side. Lokim moved with steady confidence. Treyam was forced to concede his time in exile had improved the young man. Or perhaps it was falling in love that had done the trick. In any case, his bitter restlessness, at least, now had focus.

They stopped before an ornate home, its entryway lit by glowing lanterns. With a strange twist of surprise, Treyam noticed magical elements in the building's construction – dormant now, of course. He should have expected that. The Tessilari had been instrumental in the creation of this city, even if they hadn't been welcome here for centuries.

Elle glanced over her shoulder, and Treyam nodded. Since they were all within the same passive echo spell, they could see each other. Jey and Treyam pulled the spell back so Elle was outside its reach. The girl took a deep breath and stepped forward to knock on the massive door.

For a moment, watching her, Treyam felt a wave of anxiety and disbelief. He looked at the faces around him. How was it that he, of all people, was the oldest, steadiest member of a party of such crucial significance?

As the door opened to reveal a marble hall lined in columns and glowing with lamplight, Treyam felt his lips tip up in a small smile. Life was like that, he knew. Rarely was the fate of the world placed in the hands of those most qualified to keep it safe.

The room that held the King and Queen's gathering was large, with a high, arched ceiling and a floor spacious enough to hold a much larger party than was now in attendance. A single violinist stood in an alcove by the door. The acoustics of the room carried his soft song all through the space. There were perhaps two dozen ladies and gentlemen present, dressed in their finest, arranged across the expansive floor as if placed for maximum visual impact.

Jey walked, rigid and alert, trailing after Elle with Treyam and Lokim on either side. Of the four of them, only Elle was visible to the surrounding people.

Elle's heels rang on the stone floor as she walked. She made her straight, unhurried way down the center of the room, moving unerringly towards the two chairs that sat at the top. They were large chairs, and ornate. A man sat in one. He was tall, with a strong jaw and cold, gray eyes. A woman sat across from him. Her hair done up in an elaborate tracery of gold and silver, she had high cheekbones, delicate wrists, and a mouth that seemed inclined to smile.

The two royals were alone together at the top of the room, their guests keeping a respectful distance. Jey searched the other faces, knowing the High Duke and High Dutchess were somewhere among those present, but she was unable to recognize them. For now, the King and Queen sat unattended by their respective spouses.

Quite a few heads turned in mild surprise as Elle made her journey across the large floor. She was a conspicuous presence. Her dress, while fine, was plainer than anything worn by the others here. She was also the youngest person in the room. The Queen was in her mid 40's, maybe. The King a decade or so younger.

Elle, chin lifted in determination, crossed the large room as conversation died and people turned to watch. She'd magicked her way past the guards and servants, of course, but the King and Queen did not know that. They thought she'd been admitted on her own merits.

Jey, Treyam, and Lokim stopped in the center of the room. Jey felt a mild sense of pressure as the strain of holding the passive echo spell for so long mounted. But her stamina had increased considerably in the months she'd been among the Tessilari, and sharing a spell made it easier to maintain as well. She was nowhere near the end of her strength. Treyam, she could feel, wasn't either. Nevertheless, Lokim was ready as a backup, in case one of them failed.

Elle approached the top of the room and fell into a deep curtsey. It was a graceful movement, one Jey herself could recall being schooled to perform without a hitch. Elle remained at the bottom of the bow, holding a stooped pose until the Queen said in a tone that was half bored, half annoyed, "Who has sent you, on what business?"

Jey was momentarily surprised. She'd been expecting the King and Queen to ask Elle who she was. But of course, this made more sense. They would not recognize her, so would assume she'd been sent by one of their inner circle with some sort of message.

Elle straightened. Jey, knowing her friend as she did, could see the signs of tension in her façade of poise, but her voice did not waver when she spoke. She produced a rolled scroll from within her cloak and said in a voice Lokim amplified so it rang around the room, "I am Elle, formerly known as student L134 of Tessili Academy. I bear a message from the Tessilari."

The room, which had been still before, now fell into dead silence. The violin cut off mid-song. The nobles, Jey thought, looked alert and curious, but they did not appear to understand the full import of Elle's declaration.

The King and Queen, however, did. The color drained from the Queen's face. Her eyes widened with shock. The King half rose from his chair. But he was unarmed, and the nearest guards were outside the door, stationed with their attention on the hall. If Elle had come to do him harm, she'd have killed him already.

Seeming to realize this, the man sank back. Elle added in a softer tone that Lokim did not amplify, "I am not here alone."

The Queen's hand, which had been raised in the act of reaching towards a wine goblet set on a side table, began to tremble. She moved it to her lap and folded it within her other hand. The King shifted, eyes moving restlessly among those present as if already assessing the diplomatic import of this intrusion.

At last, the Queen spoke. "What is your message?"

Elle stepped forward. The King flinched, but the Queen extended her hand, which was steady now. Elle set the parchment in the Queen's palm, and stepped away from the two chairs.

The Queen broke the seal, which let off a flash of warm light. She unrolled the scroll, and read what was written there. Her face betrayed nothing as she handed the scroll to the King. He read as well, and the two of them sat like statues for a time.

At last, the King spoke. His voice was smooth and deep and cultured. "We will need some time."

Elle curtsied again, a little less deeply than before. When she straightened, her face bore a sad smile. "Of course," she said. "But I suggest you don't take too long. The diod will take more people daily. In doing so, it will grow ever stronger."

Jey walked through the entry hatch, carrying an armful of firewood. As the narrow hallway opened into the large chamber, she marveled at how the large space had changed.

The floor was no longer covered in grit. Holdam had applied himself to helping Lokim. All the old, dead brillbane bushes had been pulled out of the ground along the far wall. Fresh soil had been hauled in and turned to mix with the old. Now, Holdam stood next to Lokim, holding a pouch of brillbane seeds and watching as Lokim set them into the damp earth one by one, closed his eyes, and caused them to sprout.

It would be several months before the plants were mature, of course, but they had instructions from the Tessilari to do all they could to prepare this place for occupation. If things went according to plan, this shelter would be a back-up. If things didn't, it might end up being the central hub of everything.

Jey walked into the vast space, watching her shadow track her as she moved. She added her load to the long stack of wood, sorting and arranging the pieces based on size. Off in the distance, she heard Elle and Biala speaking in low voices. The child, whose name was

Marim, was asleep. She'd been asleep since she'd arrived. Her tessila had not come back through the stitchring, but the girl lived on. So he must as well.

Three days had passed since they'd taken their message to the King and Queen. Three days of waiting, not knowing whether they needed to prepare to defend themselves against Masidon and the diod both, or if they would have an ally. Jey found waiting intolerable. She'd busied herself as best she could. Fortunately, there were an endless number of tasks to keep her occupied around this place.

Jey was not entirely convinced the Tessilari had done the right thing. To her, it seemed they'd played their hand too aggressively, leaving nothing in reserve. She also felt they'd forgiven too much. They'd revealed their own existence and the existence of the academy all in one go. Jey's biggest fear was the repercussions for the students behind the school's walls. What if the King and Queen decided the High Priest's little secret posed too big a threat and sent the army to destroy the place? And what about justice? The Tessilari's treaty offered forgiveness, a promise to let the horrors of the past go unaccounted for. It had not stipulated what should become of the High Priest or the handlers who had enslaved Jey and her peers. Were his crimes, then, to go unaccounted for?

Jey had seen the list of demands before it had been handed over. It had been short but comprehensive. First, the Tessilari wanted full control of the academy, as well as all texts and students. Second, they wanted a new law enacted, one that would make the killing of brillbane, tessili, or any human showing aptitude for magics into a capital crime.

In return, the Tessilari would forgive the people of Masidon for their betrayal, for the way they had murdered or enslaved anyone of magical talent for generations. Additionally, they would stand with Masidon against the diod.

Jey knew they faced a crisis. She knew asking for too much could tip the balance and cause the King and Queen to reject the treaty. Still, the thought of Nylan walking free ate at her heart like an infected wound.

Jey set the last of her wood on the stack and turned, her eyes searching the shadows that clung to the edges of the chamber. Treyam was not in evidence. He spent most of his time by the fire these last days, scribing furiously to keep up with the flood of communication being sent their way from the Valley of Mist.

Jey walked slowly across the clean floor and crouched by the sleeping child's head. Biala had found clean clothing for the girl, brushed and rebraided her long hair, cleaned her of mud and grime, and otherwise done all that could be done to make her comfortable. But the girl's condition was shocking. She was pitifully thin. Worse than that was her neck. When Jey had first seen her, a metal collar had hung there. It had chafed badly for the entire time she'd worn it, which must have been weeks. Scabs had formed only to tear open again. Several areas had been infected, oozing pale yellow puss. Treyam had healed her, but even healing magic could only undo so much damage. The girl would bear a pale silver scar around her throat for the rest of her life.

Looking at the child in the shifting sunlight, Jey rubbed at her own inner arm. This girl didn't bear the scars of hundreds of needle pricks, at least, because she was too young to have begun to go on opportunities.

Jey touched the child's forehead. It was neither warm nor cool – a good sign, she supposed. Then, with a frustrated sigh, Jey straightened and headed towards the sound of Elle and Biala's voices.

She was halfway across the chamber when footsteps sounded in the entry hatch, moving in rapid staccato. Jey turned, and Treyam swept in, his long coat flaring out behind him. His face was pale, and he held a sheet of parchment in his hand. He saw Jey, and walked to her. There was something electric but unreadable in his amber eyes.

She accepted the paper. It was an announcement, hastily printed on cheap stock, the letters slightly misaligned, the ink smeared. Jey read the headline, then looked at Treyam. He spoke, his voice a strange mix of sadness and hope. "News just reached Deramor. The diod has taken an entire village."

Jey blinked at the words, not quite able to comprehend. An entire village? Dead? In one day?

Treyam continued, voice grim. "If this doesn't sway the King and Queen in our favor, nothing will."

Jey handed the paper back to Treyam, not wanting to look at the words any longer. She finally asked a question she should have asked days before but hadn't due to a reluctance to reveal her own ignorance. "Treyam," she said, voice low, "what is a diod?"

Treyam, eyes troubled, looked away towards the fire. He blinked and shrugged. "No one really knows," he said. "So much knowledge was lost in the Two Wars." He paused, fiddling with one of the buttons on his coat. Jey waited, knowing silence was the best way to draw him out. Finally, with a sigh, he continued. "Some among the Tessilari believe they were an accident – a work of magic gone wrong. Others believe they are a weapon sent against us by another people. Whatever the case, one thing is certain. Their only purpose is destruction. Unchecked, this diod will ravage the land until there is nothing left to kill."

# CHAPTER 4

Nylan no longer walked with a limp. His body
moved with mechanical ease as he strode down the
narrow lane between the rows of small houses. His knee,
which had never recovered from the crushing blow Elle
had dealt him the night she and Jey had escaped from
the academy, worked with a smooth action.

Had Nylan been curious about this, he might have
stopped to examine himself. He might have rolled up his
pant leg and observe how his knee had changed. Where
before his right leg had been made of flesh, just like his
left leg, now it was something else entirely. The area
around the ruined joint had gone hard and solid. Blood
no longer pumped through veins. From just above the
knee down, Nylan's leg was solid as stone and nearly as
indestructible. So too was a portion of his right shoulder,
where the diod's clawlike hand had gripped him
moments after it emerged from its prison of centuries.
There were several other hard spots on his body as well.
There was a place on his left wrist where he'd been

stabbed by the young woman he'd carried back to be the diod's first meal in centuries. There was a place on his ribs where the squirming boy who'd been its second had landed a hard kick before Nylan had subdued him.

Nylan hadn't noticed the changes. He didn't notice much of anything anymore. His head was full of the whispering thoughts of the diod. He heard them constantly. They filled him with information – ancient secrets he almost, but not quite, understood. On the surface of the thoughts were desires. These desires had become Nylan's sole focus.

Generations of Tessilari scholars had debated the question of whether people taken by the diod were dead or alive. Nylan's heart still beat in his chest, and he moved freely through the world. But he no longer needed to eat. He no longer felt pain. As parts of his body ceased to function, whether through injury or lack of nutrition, they would harden, turning solid like his leg. Eventually he would become what the Tessilari called a hardened man – a creature of incredible strength, only made stronger by injury, nearly impossible to kill.

Nylan wasn't worried about these distinctions. The song of the diod was enough for him. His own thoughts, if they still existed at all, were drowned out by the constant whisper. The diod had work for him. The diod would have work for him for the rest of his days. He would work for the diod because the thought of doing anything else would never occur to him.

Right now, more than anything, the diod was hungry. It had shown incredible foresight and restraint, using the bulk of its meagre energy stores to convert Nylan instead of merely consuming him outright. For the first two days, the diod had only been able to move at a sluggish pace, drifting through the forest in its severely weakened state. But each meal Nylan provided made it stronger. Finally, it was beginning to store enough vitality to make some real progress.

They'd arrived in the first village in the middle of the night, Nylan walking, the diod stalking behind on withered legs, a creature of shadows and purple light.

They'd reached the center of the village and the diod's dark light had grown stronger. It had sent out a pulse that had locked the sleeping people around them in their slumber. From there, it had been child's play. Nylan had only to walk into each home, collect the village occupants from their beds, and carry them back to the diod.

It had taken a full day for the creature to consume the people of the first village. Then it had stumbled into the forest and woven a strange black case for itself, spitting strands of fiber from its hollow mouth, smoothing them into a solid layer with brittle hands.

Nylan, crouching at his ease nearby, had waited. Two days later, the cocoon had cracked, spilling purple light into the dawn. The diod had emerged again, smoother, stronger, and hungry. So hungry.

So they had come to this second village. Now Nylan moved smoothly, working his systematic way from house to house, pulling sleeping people from their beds and carrying their heavy, inert bodies to the moonlit town square, where he piled them in heaps to await the diod's attention.

He no longer felt fear, hunger, anger, pain, joy, or compassion, though this last had been a rare enough emotion in Nylan even before he'd been turned. He was a machine, and he worked with the single-minded efficiency of an ant carrying grass seeds back to the hive.

◈

There was panic in the streets of Deramor. Two villages, now, had been found empty, their occupants dead, left to rot in a heap in the town square. The bodies, it was said, were uncanny. The skin was gray, the eyes and fingernails black, the hair of even children gone stark white.

Rumors were flying on every street corner. Word had leaked out that the King and Queen had been warned over a week ago that this would start to happen and had refused an offer of aid brought before them.

Jey, Elle, Lokim, and Treyam were doing their part to fuel these rumors. They made frequent, brief trips into town, visiting shops, stopping to share news with anyone they could engage. They were not the only strangers in on the streets. Already, a steady stream of people trickled in from the nearest of the outlying settlements. Right now, the travelers were mostly those affluent enough to keep homes in town as well as their country estates. In time, if panic continued to spread, common people would begin to flee their homes and descend upon the capital.

All of this was happening, and still, the King and Queen had not responded to the offer Elle had delivered.

Jey was nearly mad with the waiting. When it was her turn to watch the decaying ruins of what had once been a traveler's checkpoint on the road that led out of Deramor to the west, where the King and Queen were to send a messenger with a reply, she could hardly sit still. She found herself staring down at the broken road that carried travelers towards the capital, as restless as the shifting forest light.

People were scared, and they had reason to be. The things Treyam had told Jey about the diod sounded like impossible horrors, myths made up to frighten unruly children. He'd told her any number of impossible things. A diod could trap a human in slumber. It could take a man's soul and turn him into a machine. It could drain the living of vitality, using what it took to grow ever stronger, ever faster, ever more full of dark magic.

Also, it could not be killed – not by conventional methods, at least. No weapon could land on its shadowy body. Only magic could do it any harm.

Which was why, without the Tessilari, the people of Masidon were doomed.

Jey paced around a tree and forced herself to sit, settling onto the fallen trunk that gave her a vantage of the ruined waypoint. The waypoint, like the road, was little more than a jumble of stones now, a relic of some forgotten past. What must Deramor have been like when the Tessilari had lived here as well? Great magics had once been woven into the city itself, making it almost a living thing. But those days of glory were long gone.

There was movement along the ruined road. Phril, who'd been off flying loops through the trees, returned to her suddenly, alighting on her shoulder and folding his wings, then stalking around her neck for a better view.

A mounted party was moving along the road, a long line of horses and men in armor. It was the first group Jey had seen all day that was moving away from Deramor rather than towards it. Horses snorted and pranced. Pendants hung off long poles, the colors of Masidon streaming in the mild breeze. Phril half raised his wings and let out a low, soft cry of a kind Jey had never heard him make before.

Jey rose to her feet, keeping well back in the shadows. What was this? Surely not a party sent after the diod. The settlements that had been taken lay to the north.

Jey felt her mouth go dry as the mounted men reached the crossroads. She counted quickly. The horses moved two abreast along the neglected road, but there were quite a few of them. Fifty knights, she thought, all in armor, all armed with long, glittering swords.

Understanding washed over Jey in a sick wave. The King and Queen were rejecting the offer of an alliance.

This force was their answer, an attack on the Tessilari – a violent, angry denial of the peace offering.

Jey, heart heavy, turned to go. She would need to warn the others, and they would have to decide how to respond. She took one step further into the shadows, the news she now bore weighing like a stone in her chest.

But then, a fresh splash of color caught her eye. Two horses appeared from beyond the trees, each bearing a man who did not wear armor. These men flew not the colors of Masidon, but two different crests.

First, Jey recognized the crest of the King's house, the blue and white of the House of Laws. Beside that streamed the Queen's house, the green and yellow of the House of Goods. Jey strained, looking, but did not see the red and black banner of the High Priest's house, the House of Prayers, anywhere.

Hope sprouted in Jey's heart, shouldering the heavy feeling aside. She stared in disbelief, unable to trust her eyes. For behind the men bearing the house banners rode the King and Queen themselves.

Jey watched as the mounted knights separated, pivoting their mounts and backing them partly into the trees to open a path wide enough for the men bearing the banners and the King and Queen to ride though single file. Then, the escort waited. The King and Queen rode unaccompanied to the decaying waypoint.

Jey stood in immobile disbelief for a single moment. Then, energized by nervous hope, she hurried down the slope to hear what the two most powerful people in Masidon had come out into these quiet woods to say.

◈

For the first time in 384 years, First Mage Otha let go of the mists. The spell, so long held at the edges of her consciousness, was difficult to release. Her mind had kinked around that spot like her fingers sometimes hardened around her cane. She had to pry herself free of that old, old magic, and let it go.

The mists would not fade, of course. There were younger, more agile minds to take up that work. Not all the Tessilari would leave the Valley of Mist. The alliance with Masidon was too new, too tenuous, for that.

But the Tessilari were mobilizing. All through the hidden valley, there was activity the likes of which Otha hadn't seen in ages. Old weapons were removed from storage, belongings sorted and packed or stowed away. Houses were battened down, prepared to stand empty. Perhaps forever.

The others hadn't wanted Otha to go. She was too old, they said. The journey would be too difficult. The world out there wasn't safe. It was true, the King and Queen of Masidon had signed the treaty. Magic was no longer a crime. Tessili and brillbane would no longer be hunted and destroyed. But all the Tessilari knew how good the word of this country was. They had been allies before. They could not assume this war would have an ending any different from the last.

Laws were easy to change, but the hearts of men were not.

Beyond that, news was slow to spread. While most of Masidon's population was concentrated around the capital, there were outlying settlements – places where the people may not have heard the news. The Tessilari would need to be prepared to defend themselves from the angry and the ignorant alike.

All the more reason, Otha had argued, that she leave the valley. She was, after all, the only one among them who had real combat experience.

So, at last, the younger Tessilari had conceded the point. Otha was leaving. She had surveyed the belongings in her comfortable home and been surprised at how few she wanted to take with her. As the days passed while preparations were made, she felt an escalating desire to leave. It seemed to her it had been a long time since she'd been this interested in anything.

Grip was responding to her energy, spending less time asleep and more time following her from room to room as she packed the small bag she would carry with her.

When at last Otha's party was ready to go, the last thing she'd needed to let go of was that old spell. When she did, she would no longer be the one to decide who could come and go from the valley. She was turned loose, on old woman unmoored in a strange world.

Otha insisted she go as the others went – on foot, wearing a cloak that would help her blend with the forest shadows. The only concession to her rank she accepted was the use of a small, sure-footed donkey who would carry her pack and perhaps herself if her old feet grew too sore, though she was determined not to use him for that purpose.

The party left the valley at sunrise, just as the first rays of light topped the mountain and spilled down to illuminate the mist. As Otha began to walk, following the shifting hem of High Mage Agina's cloak, the mists parted to let them through.

The Tessilari were leaving the valley. They moved through the mist, two by two, the strongest mages the race had to offer. Otha couldn't help but survey the faces of the others with some dismay. These were not the Tessilari of old. Otha could remember the men and women who'd fallen the last time the Tessilari had faced a diod. There had been Lewlin, who had carried a sword of fire and ice. There had been Elesi, whose silver tessila could grow large enough for her mistress to ride into the very clouds. And there had been Vesra, who had died in a terrible conflagration of shadow and force, using her own heart to detonate the spell that had destroyed a diod.

Otha knew that spell. She'd memorized its workings long ago. Before the surviving diod had been trapped, she had planned to use it herself, to purchase with her own life the destruction of something too horrible to be allowed to live. Other Tessilari knew the spell as well. They all did. It was taught to every child who bonded a tessila who had even the slimmest chance of being able to cast it.

The truth was, Otha did not believe the other Tessilari had the might to back the spell. Grip was old, yes, but he was powerful. He thrummed with vitality in a way the younger tessili, bred in captivity, grown to maturity in greenhouses, did not. He was the reason she was still alive. His power was what allowed her old body to go on, day after day.

And Otha had gone on for so long because, long ago, she had *seen* her own end. It would come in a burst of purple light, a ripple of titanic force, and it would bring about the destruction of a diod.

As her old feet moved in sync with the younger walkers around her and the mists fell behind, Otha felt a vast lifting on her heart. She had waited. She had waited for a long, long time. At last, it was time to die.

◈

It wasn't how Jey had expected to return. Never in even her most outrageous fantasies had she imagined a scenario where she would walk into the academy openly, through gates no longer locked, no longer topped by guards bearing stunrods.

The last times Jey had been to the academy, she'd been struck by its emptiness. The place had been built for a much larger population of students and professors than it had held in recent years. This had produced a feeling of vast quiet and solitude.

All that had changed. Jey and Elle, walking side by side, made their way through the gatehouse that stood at the end of the bridge and came to a slow stop on the other side. A courtyard stood before them. Down the slope towards the river stood the deployment blocks. A small shudder ran through Jey's body at the sight of them. Up the slope lay the faculty compound. Straight ahead stood the gatehouse and the massive wall.

The buildings were familiar, but nothing else felt the same. Where once there had been guards and orderlies and faculty, now there were Tessilari.

They seemed to be everywhere. They walked along the top of the wall, strolled across the courtyard, moved freely in and out of the faculty compound. The wall was no longer dangerous to tessili. That magic had been undone. The stunrods had been collected and stowed away. There was no longer anything here that could hurt her.

Still, Jey's feet seemed to stick at the sight of those open gates. A million memories crowded up like the remembered threads of a nightmare. Except these were not nightmares. They were real things, things Jey had been forced to do by the people who had once run this place.

The Tessilari had assembled a special team to see to the current students, to assess them and determine the safest way to wean them of their drugs. The faculty had been mostly let go. Only Professor Liam had asked to remain, saying he knew the library, knew more magical theory than any other living person. He thought he could help.

It was, in fact, the sight of her old professor that broke Jey out of her frozen position on the cobblestones. He stood, rising from where he'd been sitting on a bench outside the faculty compound. He began to move in their direction. He'd been waiting for them, Jey realized. And that knowledge helped dispel the cold dread that had begun to coil around her heart.

Phril, too excited to hold still any longer, took off. He'd spotted a cluster of tessili flying in loops just above the wall. Jey felt her heart seize as he left her, his red hide brilliant as a jewel in the clear air. Now that the spell no longer contained the tessili, they were everywhere. They danced beneath the sun, free, as they were meant to be.

Liam came to them and stopped, reaching out to clasp Jey's hand, then Elle's. Though the academy had been turned over to the Tessilari several days before, Jey and Elle had waited, giving the place time to transform. And transform, it had. The academy was now home to a significant percentage of the remains of the Tessilari. It was a strategic move as well as a practical one. The massive wall was now a barrier between the Tessilari and the population of Masidon – a barrier that would make both sides feel safer until such time as true trust was restored between them.

Liam glanced over his shoulder as two laughing boys raced each other down the river bank, careening right past the deployment blocks without even glancing at them. "I can't believe it," Liam said in a wondering tone, "I was offered the chance to go, at last, and I did not take it."

Jey wondered if the deployment blocks had been gutted, or if the walls of weapons still remained, if each still held a drawer full of syringes.

In the days since the King and Queen had come to the forest to accept the treaty the Tessilari offered, things had been happening very quickly. Although the Tessilari had not demanded it, when the High Priest's crimes had been revealed, his power had been broken, his position in government dissolved. The House of Magics, which had been disbanded around the time of the betrayal, had been reinstated. High Mage Agina was made its head, so she was now the High Mage of all Masidon, not just the Tessilari, and the third most powerful person in the country. All the seats within the house had been offered to the Tessilari. Which meant the government had been restored to the way it had been before the Betrayal.

Jey wasn't entirely sure if she was satisfied. Certainly, this was progress, but it felt too easy to be real. As she stood in the bright sunlight, rubbing her inner arm, Jey's mind swarmed with all she'd learned in recent days.

A suspicion had been growing in her day by day, coalescing as more details about the recent history of Masidon had been revealed to her. She'd tried to avoid thinking about it, but it had formed anyway. Now, she turned to look at Liam. There was more gray in his hair than in the days when she'd been his student, but he'd lost the sad air of defeat that had clung to him then.

She spoke in a sudden rush, the words tumbling out of her mouth of their own accord. "I killed other people like us, didn't I?" she said. She rubbed harder at her arm, remembering all those nights she'd ridden from here into the darkness. "They were people who would have become Tessilari if they had been allowed to live, weren't they?" She had puzzled over this question for some time. She could remember all the killing. What she hadn't been able to figure out was why? Who had she been used to systematically murder?

Liam went still, his smile fading. He'd been put in charge of organizing information since he was the only remaining person on the campus who was at all familiar with how it had run before the turnover. He would know the truth.

Now, he looked at Jey. His eyes were both somber and kind. "Everyone has agreed students are not to be held accountable for any actions they may have been forced to engage in when sent on opportunities."

Jey closed her eyes. She could remember the people whose lives she'd taken. It was the cruelest aspect of her fractured memory. The drugs and flashnodes in the academy had scrambled her ability to store day-to-day recollections. Only when she'd been on opportunities had her mind been unfettered, able to function properly.

So Jey remembered killing. She'd killed women, children, men – the young, the old, the strong. She'd been a weapon, a tool, finely honed to be precise and effective.

She opened her eyes. Liam was still watching her. She said, "I need the truth."

He sighed and looked away, his eyes straying down towards the blue river. "Yes," he said at last, his tone unhappy. "Your primary role here was to respond to confirmed reports of members of the populace who'd started to show an aptitude for magics. It is how the church kept a magical population from emerging again. You were also used for political purposes, to eliminate factions that expressed the belief that the laws against the use of magics were too harsh, and to promote the High Priest's views on other issues as well."

Jey felt Elle's cool hand slip into hers. The world seemed to dip and sway around her. For a moment, it was too much. The horror of what she'd done felt too heavy. She wanted to collapse to the grass and never get up.

Liam spoke. "You can't blame yourself, Jey. Generations of girls were used in this way, but only you accomplished the impossible. You not only saved other students from living your life, but you've now saved every child, man, or woman of the future who suddenly finds themselves able to weave a spell."

The words felt hollow to Jey. Phril, sensing her distress, left the cluster of tessili and flew back to her. He alighted on her shoulder, wings flared, spirits high. Liam watched him with open admiration.

Drawing comfort from her tessila, as she always did, Jey drew in a long, slow breath. "Thank you," she said to Liam. She gave Elle's hand a small squeeze. "I'm ready to go in now."

◈

The shelter in the hillside was no longer a place of stillness. Like the academy, it bustled with life and activity. The Tessilari had come, and they filled this place. Holdam and Biala and their granddaughter had been given a small corner at the back, away from the activity. But Jey was growing worried. The child had still not woken up.

"It all happened so fast," Holdam said. The solid man sat on a low stool, leaning back against the carved wall. Biala was on the floor, near the sleeping child. The girl's tessila had returned, at last. The small creature had emerged through the stitchring into Jey's shirt about an hour before where it had found itself trapped. It had struggled weakly for only a moment before giving up.

Jey had been in the library at the academy, reading some promising texts about weapons melding with Treyam and Liam. She'd left immediately, afraid the creature would go frantic with terror when it realized Marim was not nearby. She cupped him in her hand, gently pinning his wings to his body, remembering all the nights she'd held Shai so Elle could sneak into the academy to steal brillbane.

Marim's tessila, however, did not struggle. He lay in her grip with an air of defeat. He was a brilliant yellow in color, his head finely boned with pronounced brow-ridges and a tapering muzzle. He looked up at her with his black eye, unflinching. She couldn't tell if he was afraid or not.

Phril, for his part, was not happy. He hated it when other tessili came near Jey. The nights she'd held Shai, Phril had been furious. But now, Phril was only irritated. He sat on her shoulder, annoyed but not incensed. She could feel that he understood the necessity of what she was doing, and that he would not interfere.

That in itself was remarkable. Jey let her feelings of warmth and admiration for his newly developing temperance flow freely through their bond, making sure he knew she was happy with this new, more rational Phril. He preened a little, and made a show of not even keeping both eyes on the yellow tessila, at least not all the time, as Jey made her way back to the shelter where Marim still slept.

She found Holdam and Biala near their granddaughter, as always. She set the yellow tessila gently on the girl's chest. He seemed happy, walking up to her neck to rub his face against her jaw, then settling down on the soft skin at her throat, where he also went to sleep.

Jey watched the tessila, then said in a low voice, "Where are her parents?"

Holdam shook his head as if he could deny the past. Biala's face went dark with sadness. Holdam said, "It started with little Marim here. You know the old song, I'm sure? The song about the signs?"

Jey shook her head. She knew little about the lives and culture of the people of Masidon, even though she must have been born somewhere, the child of parents perhaps not so different from the kind cheesemaker and his wife. She could remember nothing of her life before the academy. Though she could remember missing her family, she could not so much as recall her mother's face.

Holdam began as if to recite a song, but Biala cleared her throat and touched his hand. She glanced at the space around them, which was full of Tessilari – people who had expressed an aptitude for magic and bonded with tessili. "Perhaps not here," she whispered.

Holdam's face went a little pale. He glanced up the long room. "Right," he said. "Anyway, there's a song that tells the early signs of an aptitude for magics. Some of them don't mean much now, like the tessili following a person everywhere, since there are no wild tessili anymore. But some of them are uncanny, like, and they sound like nonsense until you see it start to happen. Strange things, like feeling your mind suddenly change about something when someone touches you, or someone appearing next to you without you noticing their approach. Most of all, though, it's the hunger."

Jey blinked, shifting her gaze away from the sleeping yellow tessila to Holdam's face. "Hunger?"

Holdam nodded. "They go ravenous for a time, eating for half a dozen people yet never getting any the thicker for the extra food. In fact, they go skinny." He thrust his chin towards Marim. "She got the hunger five years ago. Her parents came to us in a panic. We thought we could hide it, since there is food aplenty at the cheesery and no one to notice how much gets eaten before it leaves us. But then the hunger came on her parents as well. They say it often happens that way, coming on a family like a contagion. We were scared to death, as you can guess. The worst came less than two weeks after they arrived. I woke one morning to find our son and his wife dead in their beds. And little Marim. Well, she was gone. We never saw her again until the night she came pounding at the kitchen door."

Holdam's eyes had gone slick with tears as he told his story. He reached out to touch Marim's hand, as if to reassure himself she was still there. Jey shuddered, wondering for a sick moment if it might have been her. Had she been the one to creep into the sleeping house, murder two adults, and abduct a child?

But no, five years ago she'd have been too young –
not yet advanced enough to go on opportunities. The
thought gave her some small measure of relief.

Jey set her hands on her knees, preparing to rise. She
was anxious to hear what Treyam and Liam were
discovering. But as she shifted she caught a strange
glimmer. It came from near Marim's chest where one of
her hands rested in repose.

She blinked and looked again, but saw nothing. The
child's wrist was thin, the skin bearing fine scratches left
from pushing through thick underbrush.

Jey felt something strange then – a desire not to look
more closely. For a moment, the magic almost worked.
She almost turned her head, almost let it go.

But Jey had been trained to recognize this type of
interference. As one part of her mind turned aside from
the curiosity, another came awake like a furious guard
hound. She snapped her attention back to the child's
wrist. This time, she saw it.

A thin chain was fastened there. She could see it
clearly now that she'd pushed through the spell that
encouraged her not to pay attention. Attached to the
chain was a pendant. "What is this?" she said, leaning
forward to a pull the object free of the girl's sleeve. It was
only a disc of flat metal, engraved with the telltale swirls
and runes of the Tessilari.

Biala frowned, blinking and staring at the bracelet. At the same time, it seemed to Jey that the thing wavered somehow, shifting as if to evade notice.

Biala's voice was low and wondering. "I never saw that before. I bathed her. I swear it wasn't there."

Jey could feel enchantment on the thing – a passive echo spell and something else, something darker. She leaned forward and undid the clasp so the bracelet fell free of the girls' wrist.

Marim gasped, her eyes flying open. With a small shriek of pure terror, she sat up.

# CHAPTER 5

The silver pendant glittered in the late light as it dangled on its chain between Liam's fingers. "It's a suppressor," the professor said. "I've read about them. They were used to force the Tessilari who built the academy in compliance. They draw power from the wearer. Marim must have been so exhausted, it was taking all her energy, making it impossible for her to wake up."

Jey felt a shudder of pure rage ripple through her. She'd brought the thing to Liam after taking it off the child's wrist. The girl, once awake, had been all but incoherent with hunger and fear. Jey left her with her grandparents and returned to the academy, finding Liam still in the library in the old faculty compound. Treyam had looked up when she'd entered, greeting her with a hopeful look. Then he'd seen her face. He'd been seated in a worn chair, his long coat pooling around him. He'd stood and taken a step in her direction.

Even carrying the thing in the pouch on her belt had been a strain. She could feel the weight of it there, dragging on her mind and her bond with Phril. She'd snatched it out and all but flung it at Liam.

Jey, too restless to sit properly, now perched on the long table that stood beneath the window. Treyam had settled back down not far off, but she was aware of a keen look in his eye as he watched her.

Some of the tired creases Jey remembered from her days in his class returned to Liam's face as he looked at the pendant. He glanced at Jey, then back at the disc. "It was one of many ways your people were coerced into orchestrating their own extermination."

Jey turned to look out the window. Outside, the academy lay in all its well-groomed splendor. The broad lawn, the sculpted hedges, the rough, rearing stone wall – it was the landscape she had known most of her life. She had vague, unspecific memories of walking serenely from class to class, of dancing lessons in the hall with the other students, and of the constant presence of the orderlies with their spritzer vials and their soothing voices, shepherding the confused, drugged students through their quiet days.

It had all been the most pernicious kind of lie. It was changed now, of course. The Tessilari were here. The walls were no longer a prison, the people within no longer captives.

Still, Jey's anger was not so easily set aside. The bracelet was just one more horror – one more despicable tool. Would no one pay for the crimes her people had suffered? Was no one to account for the death, the suffering, the loss?

"Jey?" There was a cautious note to Liam's tone. She turned to see both Liam and Treyam looking at her with wary eyes. Phril was on her shoulder. He'd half flared his wings and once again released that strange, haunting cry she'd first heard him make in the forest. He craved revenge even more strongly than she did. She could feel it in him – a desire to rend and tear, to smash the enemies that have brought his species so near extinction.

In the distance, down the slope towards the river, Jey could make out the deployment blocks. The equipment within them, she now knew, had been requisitioned. Using the texts Liam had provided, the strongest and brightest of the Tessilari were even now at work converting the contents into magical weapons for use against the diod and its monstrous army.

Jey realized with an abrupt chill that she didn't care about the diod. No. That wasn't quite right. She did care. She would join her people and stand against it when the time came.

For now, however, she had something else to take care of.

The deployment blocks were still there, reminding her of all the times she'd been sent out from here, released into the night with a purpose. She had been a shadow surrounded by darkness – a silent, stalking bringer of death.

The High Priest had been deposed. His power was broken. He no longer had any power over her. He no longer had power over anyone. He was awaiting trial.

But it wasn't enough.

A decision formed within Jey – hard, glittering and resolute. Justice, she understood suddenly, was within her power to deliver. She was a weapon. She'd been created by the very man she now longed to kill.

On her shoulder, Phril settled. He agreed with her decision. Jey settled as well, her new resolution resting in her chest, a warm, comforting, silent promise. She met Liam's eye. "I'm fine," she said. "I'm fine," she repeated when his eyebrows lowered in skepticism.

And, she discovered, as he began to speak again, explaining more about the horrid bracelet, she was fine. And she'd be even more fine tomorrow, after she'd carried out one final assassination.

◈

Treyam's first instinct upon leaving the valley had been to mistrust anyone not bound to a tessila. Now that he'd met Liam, however, he was finding the man both too useful and too likeable to be on his guard around him. When he learned Liam was responsible for facilitating Jey's escape from the academy, his respect for the man only grew.

What's more, Liam knew a good deal more about the Tessilari than anyone else Treyam had ever spoken to. He knew about types of tessili Treyam had never heard of. He knew about the sorts of strengths and weaknesses different lineages of human and tessili were likely to produce.

He also, now more than anyone, knew the truth about the academy. Treyam could see how that knowledge weighed on the man. He was in his fifties, Treyam guessed, with hair going to gray and shoulders that seemed to bow under some great weight. More strangely, he seemed to have no desire to leave. The other professors had eagerly accepted freedom when it was offered them. Not Liam. He seemed to have an attachment to the academy, and to Jey in particular.

It was a fatherly sort of attachment, Treyam reassured himself as he watched the two of them sitting together from his vantage by the window. He was finding Liam's library very useful. He also, if he was being honest, had been dogged by a strange sort of fatigue these last weeks. Nim felt it too, he could tell. She should have been off cavorting with the other tessili. Instead, she hardly left his collar. The library gave him an excuse to stay off his feet.

Treyam was trying not to worry about that and trying to convince himself that there couldn't be anything romantic about the evident bond between Liam and Jey. Still, it was a little hard that the professor could make her smile in a way Treyam himself had never really managed.

That evening, after she returned with the bracelet she'd taken from the child, the three of them resumed their work. They were searching for any references on how to destroy the armies of the diod. If Liam's research was correct, the diod would be defended by scores of humans who had once been normal men and women but whose wills had been overrun by the diod and whose bodies would no longer feel pain.

Of course, anything the three of them discovered would be passed on to those in charge. Treyam wasn't in any sort of leadership position. He could have had that, years ago, if he'd been inclined to follow in the footsteps of his forebears. When his bond with Nim had produced such disappointing results, however, he'd withdrawn to the edge of things. Many among the tessilari still watched him with a sort of strange hope, as if he might someday emerge as the remarkable leader others of his line had been. Treyam himself doubted that. Sure, he was a versatile caster. He could heal very well. He could perform basic spellwork at a high level. But his talents were nothing compared to what his parents' had been, and their skills had been mere echoes of the power of their grandparents'.

Treyam's eyes strayed to Jey. She had settled at a desk with a book Liam had given her, but she wasn't reading. Her tessili had an alert, poised look to him.

Jey was powerful. Her bond with Phril was strong, and Phril himself was magnificent. Treyam had seen him that day in the forest. The tessila had made himself larger than any other in living memory. But Phril was also broken, and something about that brokenness inhibited Jey's ability to harness his power properly.

So, Treyam and Jey both had their issues. He wondered, though, what might happen if they had a child.

It was a ridiculous thing to wonder. He hadn't so far progressed to a point with Jey that he could set a hand on her arm without making her flinch. He didn't know her lineage, of course, but he wondered. With his ancestry, her raw power, and the boost to the tessili population that would result from combining the academy's lines with the valley's lines – it seemed hopeful that he and Jey might be the first step towards restoring the Tessilari to their former glory.

Jey, sensing his gaze, looked up. He didn't look away. Her dark eyes held his for a moment, then she rose. "I'm going to head back."

So far, Jey had refused offers of accommodations in the academy, preferring to return to the shelter in the hillside instead. Treyam could hardly blame her, given her history. Still, it chafed him a little. There was so much in this library he wanted to learn, so much he needed to discover. But he also disliked letting Jey too far out of his sight. "You can stay," Jey continued, adjusting her cloak. "I can find my own way to the shelter, even in the dark."

Treyam noted the strange quirk to her lips when she said this, but he couldn't interpret the meaning. He was about to answer when the library door swung open and Lokim walked in.

As usual, the appearance of his boyhood best friend caused a roil of conflicting emotions to tumble through Treyam's psyche. Even Nim stirred, rousing herself enough to peek over Treyam's collar. Lokim, he reflected bitterly, had wooed Elle without apparent difficulty, experiencing success where Treyam encountered only failure. It was another item on the long list of points of contention that had soured their friendship for so long.

Treyam too had wanted to leave the valley. He'd wanted it for as long as Lokim had, he'd wanted it as badly as Lokim had. But he, unlike Lokim, had understood that he was young and inexperienced and that greater minds than his made the decision to keep the population hidden and secret and safe. So while Treyam had worked out the spell that had parted the mists and allowed a pathway through, he'd done it more to show that he could than of any real intention to use it. He'd shown Lokim because Lokim was his best friend, and that's what a best friend was for.

Lokim had left. Just like that, he'd gone. He'd refused to listen to Treyam's arguments against going. He'd invited Treyam to come, but his friend's refusal to accompany him hadn't stopped him leaving.

The rovers had gone after him, of course, but they hadn't brought him home. They'd given him two stitchrings and a scribis and told him to be careful. The council had ruled that all Tessilari were free, and Lokim was within his rights to leave, though many among them were unhappy with the ruling.

The whole year he'd been gone, his absence had eaten at Treyam, festering like a sore. And then word had come that Lokim had found other Tessilari and a rescue party was needed and, of course, Treyam had volunteered to go. Now Lokim was a sort of hero, but there was a coldness between the two of them. Too many things had been said that night in the mist for them to look at each other and not remember.

So, Treyam looked aside as Lokim walked into the room but looked back quickly enough when his old friend spoke. "Tintarin has been taken."

It wasn't the words that got his attention, it was Liam's reaction. The man sat up with a horrified intake of breath. "Tintarin?" he repeated. "But that's only a few hours journey from Deramor. It's the biggest outlying settlement in the north."

Lokim's face was grim. His face had hardened in the time he'd been out in the world, the softness of boyhood falling away. He spoke in a clipped monotone. "We mobilize on the morrow."

The night was wild. A high wind blew in from the south, rocking the trees and whipping down streets. Jey moved with a sense of purpose, stalking through the deserted lanes of Deramor with focused grace.

It was a good deal easier to move undetected now that she could hold her passive echo spell for a greater length of time. It was also a comfort to have Phril with her. She was aware of his eager interest as she strode around the corner of a baker's shop. It was a nice change from the undercurrent of murderous frustration she used to receive from him as he lay beneath the weighted harness the orderlies had forced Jey to put on him each time she went on an opportunity.

Jey now walked with a giddy sense of freedom and power, dropping into her old role without difficulty. How many times had she hunted out sleeping people to deliver death in the night? How many times had she brought violence to the innocent?

Tonight would be different. Tonight she would revert to her old self for only a brief time. This night, however, she would deliver justice. This night, no one but herself would choose where her lethal energies were directed.

The High Priest, she'd learned that evening, wasn't even in prison. He was being "held" in his own manor house, living in perfect ease and comfort. He was under guard, and he was not allowed to leave. Still, the injustice gnawed at Jey. This was a man who had systematically perpetrated an unending string of murders. This was a man who had turned girls like Jey into monsters. This was also the man who, if Marim's reports could be believed, Nylan had stolen a map from. That map had led Nylan and Marim to the diod's ancient prison.

As she walked, Jey's emotions seemed to coalesce and condense, forming into one sharp shard of hatred.

She knew the streets of Deramor. She'd stalked them often enough. Now she made her way towards the inner walls that led to the administrative city. The gates were closed, manned by two sleepy guards. The wind covered the sound of the shallow handholds she popped into the wall. Then she was climbing.

It felt good to use her body. It felt good to clear her mind, to narrow down to the necessity of holding herself steady, maintaining the tension in her limbs that let her climb. She moved up, popping in new handholds one by one. It was difficult to hold her passive echo spell at the same time. She'd never have been able to do it if Phril hadn't been with her.

But Phril was with her, and he was excited. He clung to the whipping end of her cloak, glorying in the mad flapping. He was staying near her, as she'd asked, but she could feel his high spirits, his barely contained desire to leave the cloak and ride the roiling air with his own wings.

Jey reached the top of the wall. She could feel the sweat standing on her forehead. She felt alive for the first time in months. She jogged forward, navigating her way down a set of narrow steps, then making her steady path into the heart of the administrative city. She passed the Queen's compound. Light spilled out of the upper windows of one tower. Jey wondered briefly who was awake on a night like this, but she didn't linger.

The High Priest's manor house was encircled by a wall, but this barely slowed her down. She climbed as she had before, then flung herself off the top, leaping towards the ground below and using a passive bearing spell to diminish the force of her fall. It was a bit of a waste. Jey could have used steps again. But she felt so strong. She felt full of life, full of energy. She felt unstoppable.

The manor was dark. Jey approached the door and forced the latch. Then she was inside, stalking through the main hall on silent feet.

The High Priest's bedchamber was not hard to find. She lifted it from the mind of the first sleeping servant she encountered. It was the sort of magic Elle was typically better at. Mental manipulation had never been Jey's strong point. But the servant girl was asleep. Jey crept to her bedside and set a hand on her forehead, using a passive persuasion spell to make her think about the chamber Jey wanted and where it was in this vast house.

Then she was on the move again. Jey dropped her passive echo spell as she approached the closed double doors. She gave Phril permission to fly. He leapt into the air with a mad surge of joy. He flew in a loop around her head as Jey opened the door to the High Priest's chambers, and stepped inside.

The latch clicked as she snugged the door shut behind her. She took several steps forward, moving into a vast antechamber with a domed ceiling. Straight ahead stood a sitting area with a set of double doors that led to a balcony. To the right stood an alcove with a massive desk and several ornate chairs.

To the left was another alcove. This one housed a sprawling bed. Jey turned, her mind going crystalline and clear with purpose. She took three steps forward, her soft shoes making no noise on the polished stone floor.

The man in the bed sat up, looking towards Jey with an expression of dull resignation. She froze, arrested by the strange look in the sunken eyes.

The High Priest spoke, his voice a sighing whisper in the still chamber. "I always knew one of you would come for me."

◈

The force of Jey's shock rippled through her, rooting her feet to the floor. She stared at the man in the bed. His hair was gray and sparse. His shoulders were thin in his night shirt, devoid of muscle. As she watched, he moved his hands out from underneath his ornate bedspread and folded them before him. There was fear in his face, but also acceptance. "You are J114, am I correct?"

The sound of that number caused a burst of anger to bloom in Jey's mind, burning some of her surprise away. For a moment, her vision was overtaken by a red haze. She wished she had a name to fling back at him, a way to refuse his label and reassert her claim on the identity the school had stolen from her. But Jey did not remember her real name, or her parents, or anything about her life before the academy. It was this man who had taken that from her, who had forged her into the weapon she was now – an assassin without a past.

Jey began to stalk forward again, drawing the two long knives that hung at her hips. She had intended to smother him in his sleep. This, she thought, would be more satisfying.

It was hard to tell in the moonlight, but Jey thought the man's face went a shade more pale. He did not move, however. He faced her, gaze steady. "I have only ever acted for the good of Masidon," he said. "Surely, you know that. Tessili are an abomination. They grant powers to mortals – divine powers that should lie only in the hands of the gods."

His words were false. Jey knew they were false. Yet, something stirred inside her as she crossed the vast floor towards the alcove. The man's face was sincere. He spoke with conviction. He was wrong, but he believed he was right.

Jey reached the foot of the bed. The grips of her knives were smooth and familiar in her hands. Phril, nearly invisible in the shadows, darted in excited loops around the room. The High Priest's eyes tracked him for a moment, then returned to Jey's face. "I forgive you, child," he said, "for taking my life."

The room seemed very still. Outside, the wind doubtless still tossed and swirled, but this room was sealed tight. There were no chinks in the window frames to let in the howling, no cracks in the walls to leak a draft. This man had lived his days in ease and luxury, cocooned in his comfortable station and his unwavering convictions.

Jey tried to guess at his tactic. Was he trying to humanize himself, attempting to change her mind by appearing weak and vulnerable? Or did he have some hidden weapon—another vile artifact like the suppressor—that he would use on her the moment she drew too near?

Well, there was no need to find out. Jey pulled strands of magic from the air, weaving them into a passive echo spell. She dropped this around herself, watching the quiver of surprise and fear in the High Priest's face as she faded from his view. She took a few steps to one side and waited, counting to thirty, watching to see what he would do.

The man in the bed stared at the spot Jey had been, then he closed his eyes. Jey slid her two knives back into their sheaths and drew a smaller knife, this one made for throwing, from its place at the small of her back. She wouldn't get close enough to find out if he had a trick up his sleeve. He wasn't moving. Her knife could find his throat from here with ease.

Jey cocked her hand, preparing the throw. The balance of her weapon was familiar. Her arm was strong. Her hand was steady. She would not miss.

"Jey, don't do this."

The voice spoke out of the darkness, making her whirl around in surprise. She watched in numb astonishment as Treyam stepped out of the shadows to one side of the bed, his long coat shifting and swaying as he walked.

She stared at her friend in a blaze of confusion. She almost lost hold of her passive echo spell. She did not understand. Was this a betrayal? Had Treyam somehow been working for the enemy all along?

Treyam continued forward. He held his staff in his left hand. Its runes were alight with coiling power. His amber eyes were colorless in the pale light, but his expression was warm – even sympathetic. "Murdering this man will not heal Masidon," he said. His voice was low and rich. "Nor will it sooth your regrets."

Jey felt her cool resolve leaving her. The bright, comforting decision she'd been carrying since Liam explained about the suppressor seemed to shatter and fall to fragments. She didn't understand. Treyam was supposed to be on her side.

"I do not say he should not be held accountable for his deeds," Treyam continued. "But his trial needs to be public. He needs to own the horrors he has committed. The whole country needs to hear what he has done. He will not walk free, Jey, but if you murder him now he will take what he knows to the grave."

Jey felt the prickle of tears behind her eyes. Treyam was right. She knew that. Her skills were not needed or wanted in the new world the Tessilari would build. Violence could beget only violence, and the people of Masidon had shed far too much blood already.

Jey let her passive echo spell fall. She returned her throwing knife to its sheath. And that's when Phril decided to take matters into his own hands.

◈

Balist, the former High Priest of Masidon and former dean of Tessili Academy, tried not to quiver as he sat in his bed and waited to discover whether he would live or die. He tried to tell himself that he was at peace. His relationship with Delari was strong. She had chosen him above all other men to head her church. He had served her well. He had seen to her people, kept them safe.

He had made mistakes, of course. He remembered that day so long ago now, when he'd visited the academy and been warned about the student, J114, who now stood at the foot of his bed with murderous intent. He should have listened, then. He should have accelerated her graduation as had been recommended.

He'd also made a mistake in trusting Nylan. When he'd discovered the existence of his bastard son, he'd felt a paternal desire to help the young man, to elevate him out of the squalor of his upbringing and help him to greater heights. That had been complicated as well. A priest was meant to have no love but for Delari. But Balist was a man. Like all men, he had made mistakes.

He hadn't known the map Nylan eventually stole would lead to the ancient prison of the diod. He hadn't known failing to eliminate J114 that day would amount to signing his own death warrant. Delari did not grant even the most exalted among her servants the gift of foresight.

Yet there were writings that indicated some among the Tessilari had such a gift. It was not natural for a mortal man or woman to see the future. So much about the Tessilari was unnatural. These people, two of them, had arrived in his bedchamber in the middle of the night, infiltrating both the administrative city and his personal defenses without apparent difficulty. He knew this was the least of what they could do.

How could the sons and daughters of Delari let such unnatural powers go unchecked? How could any normal man or woman live side by side with such people? Tessilari could control even the thoughts of others. For all Balist knew, the man at the foot of the bed was doing that even now – placing his own thoughts in among Balist's to grow and hatch like the eggs of a blight bird.

Fortunately for Balist, the man who had appeared in his bedchamber appeared to be talking J114 down. It had been a blow to learn that the work of the church, which Balist had believed so successful, had actually been incomplete. All these years the Tessilari had been lurking, undetected, just beyond his reach.

Balist watched, waiting, trusting in Delari not to abandon him at his moment of need. He watched the girl's body language shift, saw the certainty drain out of her. He almost smiled as she returned her throwing knife to its sheath.

Then there was a strange keen on the air. The small darting tessila that had been flitting about the room swept in an arc towards his bed, releasing that haunting cry. J114 gasped, spinning towards the small animal. "Phril. No!" Her voice rang in the still room, but appeared to have no effect.

There were records at the academy, works of writing that suggested the flashnodes induced a kind of madness in the tessili there. It was why the creatures became so irrational and volatile as the girls grew older. The flashnodes disrupted the connection between tessila and student, limiting the power that could be exchanged. The flashnodes, Balist knew, were the heart of what had made the academy work.

Now, Balist had a moment to regret what the flashnodes had done to this one tessila.

At first, he was not afraid as the creature darted towards him. It was tiny, after all, impotent in its fury. Then there was a blurring in the air and a tremendous crash. Balist felt his bed collapse, shattering as the tessila, suddenly the size of a horse, hurled itself at him.

Feathers flew into the air as talons scored the bedclothes. Balist felt a crushing impact on one side. He was hurled free of his bed so that he tumbled past J114 and the young man. His shoulder and head cracked against the hard stone. He slid across the ground, dazed, to come to rest in the center of the antechamber, before the doors.

"Phril, stop it." Balist could hear J114's sharp voice. He could also hear thuds and scrapes as the tessila fought its way free from the collapsed bed. His head was spinning, but he managed to sit up and arrange himself in a more dignified pose. He would not meet his death sprawled on the floor.

He looked towards the broken bed in time to see it all happen.

First, he saw the red tessila, free of the bed now and advancing on him like an overgrown, stalking cat. There was no thought in those eyes, no awareness, only lust for the kill. J114 stood by the creature's shoulder, pleading to no avail.

Then, another tessila appeared. This one darted around the large one, a mere speck in the silver air. She flew in front of J114's tessila and expanded as well, shifting to the size of a scenthound. She settled on the floor between the enraged tessila and Balist. She raised her wings.

The enormous red tessila hissed and opened his mouth, displaying rows of glittering teeth. "Phril." J114's voice was a choked sob.

And then the small tessila on the floor erupted with light. Where before her scales had been a pale blue, now they were incandescent. A brilliant glow permeated the room, so bright Balist had to raise his hand to shield his eyes. He squinted, staring with wonder. He had read of this type of tessila, but he'd thought them long extinct.

J114's tessila froze in its attack, going still as a statue. The young man appeared, stepping around the massive tessila's haunch and walking to set his hand on the glowing tessila's shoulder. He was glowing as well, giving off a light equally as bright as his monster.

Although Balist knew he should not be impressed, although he knew these magics were unnatural and corrupt, he couldn't help but feel a little swell of ... some emotion he could not quite name. Of all the powers he had read of over the years, this one seemed the most divine. Now he looked up at the young man's eyes, knowing he would survive the night. "You are a peace warden," he said. "Thank Delari."

# CHAPTER 6

The Tessilari were gathering for battle. They were a strange army. They formed in quiet clusters, men and women standing shoulder to shoulder, tessili wheeling and flying overhead in groups and swirls. In the very center, at the heart of the formation, First Mage Otha stood in silence. As the sun topped the distant mountains and fell over the valley outside Deramor, some of the years seemed to fall away from the old woman. She walked with a staff, but so did many others present. Every Tessilari now bore a magical weapon. The stunrods taken from the orderlies had been distributed among them. Jey had learned from Liam those weapons had been designed and created for use against the diod and its minions.

Jey and Treyam reached the edge of the broad field as the first rays of sun spilled down to light the army in a warm glow. Phril was small again. He'd crawled well up into Jey's sleeve and now crouched there, full of conflicting feelings. He felt remorse over his loss of control, and shame that Nim had prevented him from destroying the high priest.

In normal circumstances, Jey would have tried harder to comfort him. At the moment, she was experiencing similar confusion. She knew it had been wrong to decide to murder the high priest. She was glad Treyam had stopped her. Except something had changed between them in that bedchamber. The balance of power had shifted. Always before, Treyam had exuded an air of flippant indifference about everything. He'd seemed resigned to the fact that Jey could use his staff more effectively than he could, that her tessila was larger, stronger, faster, that she could outperform him in any physical contest. He'd never seemed to care.

Jey glanced over at the young man as they reached the first cluster of Tessilari and exchanged murmured greetings. He had stopped glowing. Nim, like Phril, was diminutive again. She was tucked into Treyam's collar, but she was no longer blue. Her scales had bleached to a pure, bright white except for pale azure accents along her brow ridges and spine.

Treyam was a peace warden. The thought repeated in Jey's head in a strange loop. Jey had never heard of a peace warden until she and Elle had fled to the Valley of Mist. There they had learned all about the War of the Diods and the betrayal. Peace wardens had never been common, but they were powerful in battle. They could call upon their tessila, bathing themselves and the area around them in an incandescent glow. All physical violence around them would fall still. No human, tessila, or animal could harm another if a peace warden was near. It was how the first diod had been defeated. A peace warden had strode to the very heart of the enemy forces, then destroyed the diod using a spell that killed her as well.

Now, Jey's heart seemed to tremble as she stole a glance at Treyam's face. He walked with a new confidence, his shoulders square, his eyes resolute.

Jey knew that spell – the one that had killed a diod. All Tessilari were taught to cast it, usually at a young age. Jey and Elle had learned it when they'd arrived in the valley.

Treyam knew it, too. And that thought somehow made Jey even more uncomfortable than the memory of the previous night. The knowledge that she'd almost done something unforgivable ate at her, yes, but it wasn't what caused the coil and swirl of anxiety to writhe in her chest.

Surely, she told herself as she followed Treyam's purposeful stride into the heart of the Tessilari forces, surely he did not intend to attempt to destroy the diod himself?

At last, they reached the center of the camp. Jey saw relief smooth the worried creases out of Elle's forehead as her friend saw them coming. She smiled, something a little sly about the expression. Her eyes flicked from Treyam to Jey and back.

They had not returned to the shelter where the other Tessilari were staying after their adventure in the High Priest's mansion. They hadn't discussed it, but by some unspoken mutual agreement they had retreated to Lokim's old hideout instead. Treyam and Jey had slipped inside, built a fire, and fallen asleep side by side. They hadn't spoken. In the night, Jey had felt an understanding between them. She'd been confident he wouldn't tell anyone what she'd nearly done.

Now, in the light of morning, Jey wondered if she'd been foolish and naïve, imagining that shared feeling of connection in the darkness. Perhaps Treyam had only stayed with her to keep an eye on her, so he could deliver her to the hands of those who would judge and punish.

Elle opened her mouth as if to speak, as if to make some remark about the fact of Treyam and Jey appearing together after going missing some time in the night. But First Mage Otha turned her old head, her sharp, inquisitive gaze snapping onto Treyam with sudden intensity.

Treyam set the end of his staff against the ground. He looked at Otha. Some ghost of his trademark grin lingered about his eyes. "Otha," he said. "We have a peace warden at last."

Then Nim leapt out of his collar, beat a circle around his head, and began to glow.

◈

The knights arrived two hours after dawn. They rode up in two gleaming columns, mounted on their armored horses, battle standards flapping and cracking in the air overhead. High Mage Agina stepped forward to confer with a general. Then the strange army moved out.

Jey walked between Elle and Treyam, her heart heavy as lead. Around her, the Tessilari marched in silence.

News of Treyam's transformation had traveled quickly. Now he walked beside her, head high, Nim riding his shoulder with her wings half spread. All around, people cast admiring looks in his direction.

But in front of Treyam, First Mage Otha tramped with a quick step. Just as Jey had feared, Treyam had offered to go alone, to try to bring down the monster by sacrificing his own life. First Mage Otha had refused to hear of it. "We are weak," the old woman had snapped. "Even you with your new power, we are mere shadows of the Tessilari of old. It will take all of us to stop the diod this time."

So, they walked together – a hodgepodge of men and women, young and old, powerful and weak. The gleaming knights surrounded them. Together, they crossed the broad valley and continued into the forest, breaking into smaller formations to move among the trees. Jey was grouped with Otha, Treyam, Lokim, Elle, and four other stern-faced Tessilari.

The strategy was a simple one. The bulk of the forces would engage the hardened men the diod had created, buying time. This one unit, Jey's, would attempt to push through the gathered forces and reach the diod.

Would it work? No one could say. But they had to try. The most recent reports counted those the diod had slaughtered in the hundreds. Dozens more common people had become the warriors the Tessilari called hardened men. At this rate, it would take only a few more days before the diod was unstoppable.

They walked through the quiet forest for a long time. There was little conversation around them. Jey followed on Treyam's heels, watching the dancing hem of his long coat. She wanted to speak to him, to explain herself, to tell him she didn't want him to die. She remembered that day, so long before, when she had decided to trust him, to follow him to the valley. Ever since, she'd been aware of the way he watched her. But she'd kept her distance.

Now Treyam moved straight ahead, not sparing a thought for her. She could see his determination in the set of his shoulders. She felt a strange desire to touch his arm, to make him stop and look at her, to take his hand

and lead him away. They could flee to the Fog Isles, perhaps, or somewhere beyond. It might be years before the diod's forces caught up with them.

Ahead, the trees began to thin. Off to the right, a horse whinnied as a knight commander gave a shout. Then they were moving out of the forest, stepping into another, smaller valley. The settlement of Tintarin lay below, a cluster of small houses in the morning light.

And drawn up before the houses, waiting, stood the hardened men.

They were like no men Jey had ever seen. They stood as still as stones, faces devoid of emotion. They carried a random assortment of weapons, ranging from clubs to knives to staffs to swords. They wore the clothing of tradesmen and laborers and farmers and thieves. They were the common folk of Masidon, transformed into nightmares. Some of them bore visible wounds, gashes or cuts or dented skulls. But the wounds did not bleed. The men stood shoulder to shoulder. Not a one moaned or twitched or betrayed pain of any kind.

In the heart of the village, Jey knew, the diod lurked. From their vantage point she thought she could make out a strange stain of purple light emanating from the town square.

At last, Jey felt that strange peace settle over her. Her worries about Treyam vanished. Her fatigue from the night before faded away. She felt primed, prepared, and ready. This one last time, Jey would do what she was so good at.

She drew her knives. These were new knives, handed to her this morning by a Tessilari with a gray beard and kind eyes. Like Treyam's staff, they glowed with a tracery of runic markings. She could feel the magic in them as her palms settled onto the smooth wooden grips.

The hardened men could not really be killed. Jey knew this. But they could be crippled to such an extent they could no longer attack. Magical weapons made that easier.

First Mage Otha stopped. The Tessilari formed up, the knights gleaming at their flanks. The hardened men did nothing. They only stood, a solid wall between this army and the diod.

First Mage Otha spoke, and her voice rang in the quite air. "It is time."

One of the knights raised a horn to his lips. A note sounded, high and pure. Another note answered from the end of the line. Then, the armored horses charged.

◈

Behind them, people were dying. The air was full of horrible noises, of screams, the ring of weapon on weapon, and the sick crunch of weapon on flesh. Horses whinnied, men bellowed, women cried out. The Tessilari and the knights were fully engaged. There was no turning back now.

But Treyam was glowing again. He was holding back, Jey could feel, conserving his energy. He walked in the center of their formation, supporting Otha with one arm. Around those two, Jey and her companions strode, weapons out, eyes alight with battle fervor. It had taken them only a few moments to push through the front lines. Now the small group hurried for the heart of the city, knowing every moment cost lives.

Jey still held her knives, but she could not use them. Treyam's peace warding surrounded her, suppressing any desire she might have to do violence. It was a strange feeling, and she fought it a little as they walked through the deserted streets. What if something went wrong and she needed to defend him? She would dash ahead, she decided, and move beyond his range of influence.

They hurried, the sounds of the battle falling beyond. Jey was aware that a few shambling shapes followed –

hardened men who had noticed the group push through. But they hung back, affected by Treyam's glow, unwilling or unable to come too close. Phril kept an eye on them as Jey continued, hissing.

They reached the town square at last, walking out the mouth of a street that opened onto a broad plaza with a fountain at the center. Not so long ago, this would have been a lovely place. The green was extensive and well-groomed, the paved common area wide and dotted with trees and benches.

Now it was a place of horror. Jey nearly choked on her shock when she saw the heaps of bodies. They lay in massive stacks, humans tossed into mounds like felled trees. The dead were pale, bleached of color, and utterly lifeless. Men, women and children were tangled together, whole families wiped out.

Jey felt the familiar rage begin to burn in her chest. She looked towards the center of the square. And she saw the diod.

Or at least, she almost saw it. She was aware of a shape – a tall, narrow form, shrouded in shadow, cloaked in a purple darkness that seemed yet to glow. She felt it, too. It tugged on the threads of magic in the air, coiling them into itself, turning them to poison. It held the prostrate body of a child in one clawed hand.

As Jey watched, frozen with disbelief, the diod tossed the child aside. There was movement near the fountain, and a figure stirred. It walked to the child, picked it up, and carried it to the stack of bodies.

Something about the way the figure walked made Jey look again. A strange shock of recognition shot through her. The man who so casually flung the child onto the stack of bodies was Nylan – the handler who had killed Kae – the man Jey hated most in the world.

She almost broke formation, almost dashed across the paving stones to ram her knives into his chest. It was only Elle's hand on her shoulder that kept her still, the little burst of soothing emotion her friend transferred to her with a light touch.

There would be time for Nylan later, Jey told herself. For now, they faced the diod.

And the diod, it appeared, was aware of them. It was turning, its body rotating within its supernatural cowl. It had no face that Jey could see, but there was a darkness within the purple shadows that oriented on them, seeming to focus.

Treyam began to walk, leading the group forward. The white light he gave off grew stronger, more intense, more brilliant. First Mage Otha's staff had also begun to glow. Jey felt the weaving of a great spell forming in the air around her. Behind them, the hardened men skulked, unable to come any closer.

It was going to work, Jey thought. They were going to do it. The diod didn't know to fear them. It only stood, silent and terrible, at the center of the destruction it had wrought.

A movement caught Jey's eye. She turned her head. Nylan had turned from the pile of bodies to regard their small group. His face, which had never been friendly, was now a twisted snarl of inhuman hatred. He stooped, reached into his boot, and withdrew a knife. He moved so quickly, Jey barely had time to react.

It dawned on her what he was about to do. He should have been too far away. He was beyond the glow of Treyam's peace warding, all the way across the plaza. But something about the way his shoulders rippled as he moved told her he was no longer merely a man. Nylan had changed. She somehow knew he would have both the range and the accuracy to take Treyam down.

Jey didn't think. She didn't hesitate. She charged forward, leaving formation, dashing across the cobbled stones. She reached the edge of Treyam's light. As she dashed across the hard stones, Phril erupted, expanding to a size so vast she couldn't quite take it in.

The hardened men at the mouth of the street charged Phril, dashing in with their knives and cudgels and axes, hacking at his brilliant scales. But Jey had eyes only for Nylan, and the knife he threw. It sailed through the air, turning in a lazy spin, flying straight for Treyam's exposed back.

◈

It was falling apart. First Mage Otha felt the chaos coming. The girl, Jey, left first. She leapt out of her position and hurled herself into the path of a thrown knife. For a moment, it looked like the weapon would hit her in the chest. If it had, it surely would have killed her.

But Jey swiped one of her own knives through the air, knocking the thrown knife aside. Then she advanced on the hardened man before her while those behind fell on her tessila.

Around her, several other tessilari left the protection of the peace warding, moving to engage enemy forces. Otha had to remind herself to let them go. They had come for this precise purpose. They were not hers to protect any longer.

The diod loomed before her – a pulsing, malevolent presence. It was full of the dead, replete on the stolen energies of the people who had perished here. Otha felt her own hatred snake through her, combined with Grip's. This thing was an abomination, a corruption of all that was good and right about magic. Her purple tessila was nearly young again with his enthusiasm for their final duty. He was strong in her mind, full of power and joy. For a moment, Otha regretted the end she was about to deliver unto them both.

She continued her weaving, calling magic up out of the air, out of the earth. She felt the power build within her, thrumming between her and Grip, more than she had ever held before.

Next to her, there was a sudden clap of magic. One of the other tessilari had cast the detonation spell. It went off, blasting the man out of existence, ripping a yawning gap into the magical fabric of the world.

A brilliant light formed around the diod, then shattered. The monster did not so much as flinch.

The diod, unaffected, stood taller as the man and his tessila collapsed into an inert heap, dead.

Otha cursed under her breath. The others had been told to wait, to try to take the diod only if she failed. This man, perhaps in a heroic gesture, had cast his spell first. But he hadn't been strong enough.

The diod lifted its head, an enraged bellow rising from its strange, hollow face. Before it had been only curious about them. Now it was angry.

Otha was out of time.

Her spell was ready. She could feel it on the air. She made the final weave and sent Grip one last thought, full of the boundless love she felt for him.

Then she let go.

The spell was so powerful it seemed to rock the world. It was the most magic she'd ever released, the most powerful casting she would ever work. Otha saw the light gather around the diod, and she could feel, this time, it would be enough.

Before Otha died, the sight came on her one last time. She saw the girl, Jey, and the young man, Treyam. They stood together in a courtyard full of flowers and tessili. They were holding hands and looking into each other's eyes. They would join, Otha saw, and their joining would bring a child into this world. This child would bond with a tessila. The tessila would be a strong cross between the bloodlines of the valley and the bloodlines of the academy. The child would only be one of many such crosses, but she would be the strongest. She would be a Tessilari so powerful her name would echo down through the ages. She would lead her people back to their former glory.

With this death, this sacrifice of her own life as well as Grip's, Otha was allowing that future.

Otha closed her eyes. She felt her old heart split, both with the power she had just released and with the joy that came with knowing she had carried out her purpose, at last.

◈

Jey lay in a soft bed. For a moment, her mind was suspended just before waking. She was aware she was warm and comfortable, and Phril was nearby. Her tessila was pleased with himself about something. He perched on her headboard, preening.

But Jey was confused. She hadn't slept in a bed like this one – large, soft and downy, since her years in the academy.

The thought made her sit up. Her drowsiness vanished as fear shot through her like a malevolent spell. She glanced around the large room where she now lay. Sunlight spilled through high windows. Beyond the glass, the academy grounds lay in all their well-groomed splendor.

For one horrible moment, Jey thought it had all been a dream. She had never left here after all, never broken out, never lived in a cheesery, never met Lokim and Treyam and gone to the Valley of Mist. She was a prisoner, just like she always had been and always would be.

There was a movement on the other side of the room. "Ah, you're awake." It was Elle's voice. Her friend rose from a small couch and picked up a tray. The tray bore an arrangement of breakfast foods. *Just like when I'm back after an opportunity.*

Jey's panic was a living thing now, a caged tessila in her chest, clawing to escape. Elle continued across the room, carrying the tray. She stopped when she saw Jey's expression. "Heaven's Jey, what's wrong? Don't you feel all right? Treyam said he healed you but you might be disoriented when you first woke up, because of the blow you took to your temple."

*Treyam.* Jey's panic began to fade, but she shook her head. She couldn't remember any head blow.

Elle crossed the room and set the tray on the bedside table. "Treyam insisted you needed some privacy and a proper place to sleep. You're in the faculty compound. He was here all night, by your side. He only stepped out a moment ago. He'll be back soon."

It came back in a rush, then – the diod, the battle, the massive spell Otha had cast. The old woman's magic had seemed to rip a hole in the very fabric of existence. And also, there had been Phril. He'd been fully the size of a house, smashing and raking at the hardened men that had begun to pour out of the street into the courtyard.

And Nylan. She'd stabbed him with her knife, right in the neck. He'd only smiled and driven a fist into her side. She'd been stunned for a moment and had taken another blow in her shin. But she'd rallied, infusing her knives with magic and going back on the offensive.

"The diod," Jey said. "Did we win?"

Elle handed Jey a warm mug of tea. "We won," Elle said, "if you can call it that." Her friend's eyes were sad as they rested on Jey's face. "We lost a lot of Tessilari, Jey. Treyam had to be forcibly removed from the field. He'd have killed himself trying to heal them all."

Jey felt a strange lurch in her chest. "But he's ok?" she said. "Unharmed?"

"Yes, he's only tired. Lokim too. Otha is dead, of course. Many knights fell as well. Fortunately the hardened men stopped fighting when the diod went down. Now they sit or stand where they were when it died, like strange, half-living statues. It's uncanny."

"What about Nylan?" Jey said. She could remember the fight now. She remembered infusing her knives with magic until they glowed as if fresh from the forge. She remembered landing blow after blow after blow to no avail. He'd only continued to smile.

And then …. she froze with the teacup halfway to her lips, turning to look at Phril. Her tessila regarded her with his black, dewdrop eye.

Elle spoke. Her friend's voice was cautious. "Nylan. Well. You see …." Her friend broke off, laughing a little. "Phril ate him."

Jey knew it was true. She could feel it in Phril's self-satisfaction, and the memory came back. Nylan had delivered a crushing blow to her head, smashing her down to the ground. Just before her consciousness had faded, a massive red head had struck from above, jaws closing around Nylan's body.

She turned to her tessila again, this time in concern. "Is he okay?" Jey said. "Aren't tessili vegetarians?"

Elle giggled. "He seems fine. We kept a close eye on him after he shifted. But he's been in a fabulous mood, not even hissing at Nim when Treyam healed you."

Jey reached out and ran her finger along the sharp line of Phril's jaw. "I can't believe you," she said in a wondering tone.

The door opened, and Treyam walked in. He saw Elle by the bedside, saw Jey sitting up. For a moment he closed his eyes in pure relief. Then he was crossing the room, Elle was stepping aside, and he was sitting on the bedside, holding one of Jey's hands in both of his. He looked at her with his amber eyes, Nim peeping out from within his collar. "You're awake," he said.

Jey, out of reflex, almost drew her hand away. But then she went still. It was over, she realized. The diod was fallen. The academy was free. The High Priest would stand trial for his crimes. The knights of Masidon and the Tessilari had stood shoulder to shoulder and faced a common foe. Even Nylan was dead.

Which meant Jey no longer had to prepare, no longer had to plot, no longer had to seek revenge.

Still, it was strangely hard to let go. Jey sat for a moment, blinking in the bright light. Revenge, she realized, wasn't about violence. Revenge wasn't about killing. Her revenge was just starting. She would have it by turning her back on her past. She would have it by rising above what had been done to her. She would have it by starting over and building a new life.

Jey set her teacup down. A strange feeling of peace pooled inside her. It wouldn't always be easy, she knew. The galaxy of scars on the inside of her elbow would never fully fade. She would have bad days when she remembered what she had done. She would always hate those memories.

But for now, it was morning. The sun was up. Phril was near her and happy. They were free.

Jey turned to Treyam and set her hand on top of his.

# Brinlin Isle

*Annals of the Brinlocks : Book I*

Robin Stephen

## PRELUDE

The fog was alive and thrumming with dark energy. As lightning snaked and danced in the sky overhead, the fog coiled and looped like the flight path of a maddened tessila.

Marim knelt on the narrow path that led from Lan Dinas down to the shores of the warmlake, staring ahead into the gray air. She could taste the fog—its rusty tang—but couldn't see more than a few feet in any direction. It was like being utterly alone on her own private, half-made planet.

She could feel the creeping coolness as her skirts soaked up the pooling dew and mud. She blinked and rubbed her eyes, but it didn't help. The fog muffled everything. She blinked again, swaying.

Marim was tired, and growing cold. The wind blowing ahead of the storm traced probing fingers up the nape of her neck. She shivered, her nostrils full of the scent of damp, cool earth.

Kix was upset. She could feel him flying above her, wheeling and circling in aimless loops. It was often this way for her tessila. Strong emotion overwhelmed him, made him directionless and incapable of focusing. Confused by her exhaustion, he flung himself about in the empty sky in an orgy of purposeless activity.

Marim should get up. It was strange of her to be kneeling in the path like this as the storm drew near. Nothing was finished yet. Her help might be needed. Time was running out.

Strangely, though, Marim could not get up. Her limbs felt heavy, as if they'd been poured full of wet sand. Even her heartbeat felt sluggish, as if her blood had grown thick as oil. But next to the slowness, a sense of urgency beat through her like the throbbing rumble of a distant drum.

She must get up.

Marim did not move. It felt like she'd been kneeling on this damp path most of her life. She could hear nothing but the strange hiss of the fog, see nothing but the roiling gray mists. She was having trouble remembering how she'd come to be in this place. Not just on the path, but in this fog-filled world. Her memory was as fuzzy as the blank air.

"Lan Dinas. Cynnes Tarth." She spoke the words aloud, startling herself. The names, she felt, should hold some significance. As it was, they existed like she did – cut off from everything that might give them meaning.

Kix wheeled ever higher in the thick air. Marim drooped. She didn't have to stay sitting, she realized. She could lie down and let her head nestle into the soft grass. She could uncurl her legs and stretch out and rest. She would. In a moment, she would.

She heard the thump of a boot on grass. She looked up to see a shape looming over her. She caught the scent of hair oil and boot leather, saw a pinprick of gleaming gold against a neck scarf.

A thought leapt into her head. *He's come back. He's come back, and he's going to kill me.* The certainty uncoiled from the secret place in her heart where the fear and anger had ridden since that terrible day, long ago, when she'd run into the forest, chased by the sound of screams.

She *must* get up.

She had run away that time. She needed to do it again. Then, she'd been hungry and weak and terrified. Now, there was something wrong in her mind. She was confused, not remembering properly, and Kix was so high up there, flying on the looping currents of wind she could not see.

Marim didn't move. The man loomed. Hands closed around her throat. Tight, rough hands that squeezed with precise, deliberate pressure. She had the absurd thought that at least, with his hands around her throat, he would not be able to see her scars.

The world, already gray, began to go dark around the edges.

# CHAPTER 1

The fog clung to the lines and rigging of the tidy merchant vessel, muffling the snap of the sails. It was a damp, restless haze with chilly fingers that crept in at collars and cuffs. It seemed to be growing thicker by the minute, blotting out sight and sound alike.

Marim stood on the deck, hands resting on the rail, staring into the gray air. She could hear the restless waves churning against the prow and feel the rolling of the deck beneath her feet. Over the last two months, she'd grown accustomed to the sounds and sensations of being at sea. She'd also grown used to the view. She'd been staring at the distant horizon for days, that brilliant line where blue sky met blue ocean. Now, she could see only a short distance beyond the rail.

As she strained into the fog, shapes loomed. A man on deck gave a cry. There was an answering call and a thump, then the ship began to bustle with activity. Marim moved off the rail and stood snugged up against a storage crate. She'd been told early on this was a spot she could occupy without getting in the way.

More shapes materialized on the dim air. A smaller vessel appeared down below, ready to guide them into the harbor. Ropes were thrown, men climbed over the rail. Behind her, Marim heard laughter and conversation.

Her heart, already heavy, grew leaden.

"I guess we're here." Marim spoke the words under her breath, but Kix couldn't hear. He was on the other side of the stitchring she wore on its thin chain about her neck. Which meant he was miles upon miles away in the sunny gardens of Tessili Academy, dozing on his brillbane bush.

Not that her tessila would have been any comfort if he had been with her. Kix was erratic, even by tessila standards. Marim's relationship with him was volatile at the best of times. Still, whenever she grew scared or lonely or uncertain, she reflexively wished for his presence.

There was more laughter in the dim mist and a resounding thud and shudder as the ship snugged up to a pier. A smell of overripe fish rose on the briny air, thick and cloying. In no time at all, the vessel was made fast, a gangplank was run out. They had landed in Cynnes Tarth at last.

Marim's journey was over. It was time to go.

Still, she stood by the crate. She knew she should return to the closet-like cabin she'd been assigned when everyone had thought she was going to become a permanent member of the crew. She should sling the ridiculous sea bag she'd traded her trunk for over her shoulder. She should go ashore.

But she couldn't. Marim felt stuck. It was as if her feet were nailed to the deck as surely as the furniture in the captain's cabin. She no longer wanted to be on the ship. The events that had unfolded over the last three weeks had been deeply unpleasant. Had she been a different girl, with a different history, they would have been the most unpleasant of her life. But Marim had lived through far worse.

Still, she also did not want to go ashore and face this place.

Trying to stir herself to action, Marim ran a hand through her damp hair. It was short – short enough it wouldn't fall into her eyes. It was an unfashionable cut. She'd had to argue with the barber to get him to do what she asked. When he'd given in at last, she'd felt a heady thrill at the cold touch of the shears as they snipped along at the base of her neck. Her long, dull hair had fallen to the floor. She'd felt reborn.

She'd been excited then, full of misguided hopes and expectations. This journey had been meant to redeem her, to set her on a new path.

It hadn't worked out at all the way she'd planned.

There was the ringing tramp of booted feet approaching. Captain Tommin's burly outline approached, made pale by the fog. He was a kind man. Ever since the night everything had gone so wrong, he'd assumed an apologetic air when he spoke to Marim, as if what had happened was his fault.

He stopped well away from her. None of the men came within several feet anymore. He cleared his throat and spoke in an overly hearty tone. "We're ready to take you ashore, young miss."

*And abandon me to my fate*, Marim added silently. Her heart skittered with anxiety. Panic swelled within her. *They're really going to do it*, she thought. *They're going to leave me behind.*

For a moment, Marim felt the old helpless rage. It bloomed through her like poison, filling her blood with heat, making her vision go red at the edges. She felt Kix stir, coming out of his doze. She needed to get ahold of herself, or he'd come blasting through the stitchring and make everything worse.

With an effort, Marim contained her emotions. She forced her face into a smile. "Thank you, captain. I'll go and get my things."

# Your Turn

Dear Reader,

First, I want to thank you for joining me on Jey's journey. I hope you've enjoyed getting to know her and the other characters in this series as much as I have.

Second, I am hoping you might take a moment to let me know what you thought of this series. I love hearing from my readers. You can email me at author@robinstephen.com. Or, if you're feeling very generous, you can post a review on Amazon to let others know you liked it.

If you'd like to know about my upcoming releases, you can join my mailing list and robinstephen.com.

Most of all, thank you for reading!

Best,
Robin

# About the Author

Robin has always been enamored with magic. When she was a child, that meant reading books. When she was a slightly older child, it meant trying to write her own. She produced her first attempt at a fantasy story at the age of 10. It was an unintentionally blatant (and considerably less well executed) rip-off of *The Lion, the Witch, and the Wardrobe.*

Fortunately for everyone, Robin's stories have gotten a little more original over the years. She currently lives in Iowa City, where she hangs out with her husband, trains horses, and writes.

learn more at robinstephen.com

# Robin also writes contemporary western romance

If you like horses, love stories, and the desert, explore Robin's work under the pen name Stefani Wilder. Her book, *A Man Who Rides* is available now.

see stefaniwilder.com for details

www.ingramcontent.com/pod-product-compliance
Lightning Source LLC
Chambersburg PA
CBHW070330130626
46556CB00007B/2797